HEAR MY VOICE O NEBULA

THE DESTINED UNIVERSE BOOK ONE

MIN HYESUNG

HEAR MY VOICE O NEBULA

THE DESTINED UNIVERSE BOOK ONE

MIN HYESUNG

poppypub

Hear My Voice, O Nebula (The Destined Universe Book 1)
Copyright © 2021 by Min Hyesung
All rights reserved.
First published in Korea in 2021 by Gravity Books.
English translation rights arranged with Gravity Books.
Translation copyright © 2022 by POPPYPUB LLC

Translated by Alex Lee
Published by POPPYPUB, Fort Lee
www.poppypub.com
poppypub is a trademark of POPPYPUB LLC.

Library of Congress Control Number: 2022934423

ISBN 978-1-952787-16-4 (paperback)
ISBN 978-1-952787-19-5 (ebook)

"... There will come a time

when our descendants will be amazed

that we did not know things that are so plain to them...

Many discoveries are reserved for ages still to come,

when memory of us will have been effaced."

— Seneca, Natural Quaestions

Part I

Hear My Voice, O Nebula

1.

A week ago, the Planetary Alliance Command had captured the Discarded Resistance's flagship *Okayama* from the far side of the moon orbiting Valhalla, the fourth planet in the Behemoth planetary system, within the Desirée star system. And three days ago, the command center had dispatched agents equipped with a cloaking field and EMP on the assault cruiser *Little Boy*.

The deployed agents stood in the dark airlock, readying for their mission. They were affiliated with the Third Regiment of the Alliance Defense Command, otherwise known as the Hound Dog Squadron.

"Loading ammunition," ordered Captain Yeonsu.

Indifferent eyes stared back at him. One-eyed Kirox, Lu Xun, Aiden, and about twenty other commandos. These boys were accustomed to the blood and gunfire of the battlefield; they had been turned into soldiers before becoming men. The unique sound of the Union-standard firearms reloading echoed throughout the room.

Yeonsu moved to face the group and raised his voice. "This is the moment we've all been waiting for. These are your orders."

Rifleman Lu Xun popped his gum, chewing loudly.

"Charge their ship and kill everything in sight. Then enter the bridge as quickly as possible and find the Raven." Yeonsu paused, peering around at each young man. "We cannot let the Raven fly any longer. Today, we will break those hideous wings for good."

Kirox's single eye glowed red through his goggles.

Yeonsu exclaimed, "What are you?"

"Hounds!" the Hound Dog Squadron replied.

"Bite into the enemy's neck!"

The boys grinned back at him and cried, "Devour their intestines and drink their blood!"

Ki, an engineer on the *Okayama*, was having a very bad day. Engines three and five, which were in charge of running electric power to the flank, had started flickering a day ago. Not a good sign. Moreover, the senior engineer had been off duty for over two days. Ki hadn't had a wink of sleep, since someone had to cover the shift. The chief engineer had promised him two days off after this seventy-two-hour shift, but at the fifty-fourth hour, he decided he couldn't put up with this any longer. "Fucking hell," he muttered. "At this rate, I'm gonna be crawling into a coffin."

He needed to get a few hours of rest or he was going to be useless as an engineer. As he stood up to head for the sleeping quarters, his spine cried for help. He gritted his teeth, hunching over.

At that moment, Ki saw something strange.

A green dot was shining on one side of the engine room

bulkhead. Ki stared at the dot, his brow furrowing. What could this be? He had never noticed it before.

The dot grew larger. It mocked Ki like the devil's eye. *You're fucked now, Ki. You're really fucked now—*

His eyes widened in alarm.

"Holy shit!"

The bow of the *Little Boy* broke through the *Okayama*'s outer frame and engine room bulkheads with a roar.

The interior of the engine room was transformed into rubble and garbage that no longer had any function. The bulkhead had been completely pierced through, and the gap was occupied by the pointed, triangular bow of the Planetary Alliance cruiser. Debris and oxygen were spilling out through the surrounding gaps.

The airlock located at the bottom opened wide, and heavily armed soldiers began pouring in. The Hounds took their positions. While Lu Xun and the other riflemen stood in the front row, Signal Officer Aiden began setting the photon frequency. Warning lights were flashing red throughout the ship, and alarm bells blared.

Yeonsu appeared at the end of the flank of soldiers and looked around at the engine room, crumpled like a piece of paper. Turning his gaze from a tattered corpse lying to the side, Yeonsu spoke to Aiden.

"Is it finished?"

After a moment, Aiden nodded. "It's done, Captain. They'll be coming soon. Armored droids."

Yeonsu raised his hand. Kirox and three men were spread out on both sides of the room in pairs.

The engine room's shield door opened to reveal the battle droids. Each were armed with small machine guns.

Yeonsu spoke softly. "Smash them, Kirox."

The droids pointed their guns at the troops. Kirox threw a grenade into the air. Several more followed from the rest of the Hounds.

The grenades landed near the droids.

The EMP field unfolded, drawing dizzying patterns on the bulkheads and shielding doors. The droids collapsed with a mechanical sound. Their control system had been disabled. Yeonsu gave a signal with his hand. The riflemen passed through the shield door where the had droids entered, and the captain and the rest of the troops followed.

The *Okayama*'s armed forces crossed over from the cabin area to defend the ship, but they were shot and killed before they could resist. Yeonsu ordered Kirox to place the battle droids at the entrance to the cabins.

Enemy riflemen met Yeonsu at the front of the bridge. *Okayama*'s troops and the Hounds stood in confrontation. Yeonsu was about to give the order to fire when a familiar face caught his eye. Stepping forward, he waved his hand at the man armed with a pistol.

"Hello, Captain Byungwook."

Captain Byungwook of the *Okayama* glared back at him.

"It's nice to see you," continued Yeonsu. "Although the situation is not ideal. How have you been?"

Byungwook spoke carefully. "I've been fine. Until your troops raided our ship."

Yeonsu shrugged. "You don't like my greeting? I tried to be as polite as possible. That's too bad."

Byungwook gritted his teeth. "What do you want? Why have you brought the Hounds to attack my ship?"

"What do I want? The fact that you, the former commander of the Alliance, are now the captain of this ship should explain why we are here without me spelling it out for you. To give you a reason, number one: the Alliance has discovered that this ship is a flagship of the Discarded."

Byungwook's mouth pinched at the sides.

"Number two, and the ultimate reason, is that there is a White Raven aboard this ship." Yeonsu aimed his rifle at Byungwook. "So, traitor, tell me. Where did you hide that damn Raven?"

Byungwook knew there was no getting out of this alive. The Hounds had him and his crew surrounded, and at any moment, Yeonsu could annihilate them in the blink of an eye. But his mind was occupied by something other than the life and death of his crewmembers and himself. It was the same thing he guessed was causing a sense of urgency for Yeonsu as well.

The reason why Yeonsu was talking to him instead of killing him straightaway was because he did not know the whereabouts of the White Raven.

Byungwook wet his lips and decided to stall a little longer. "General Yeonsu. You also come from the Mining Guild. You being an officer for the Alliance is a comedy in itself. Do you know why the Mining Guild fell?"

Yeonsu frowned. "What are you trying to say, Captain? If you're trying to buy time, it's pointless."

Lowering his pistol, Byungwook stepped out in front of the riflemen. "It's not a bluff. I joined Discarded because I received definitive intelligence that the Alliance played a key role in the downfall and destruction of the Mining Guild."

Yeonsu narrowed his eyes. "Cut the bull."

"You don't believe me? I didn't at first, either. But hear

me out; I have information that will make you think other-wise," Byungwook said in a firm voice. "It was the Alliance that created the Big Crush."

"Keep up the bullshit and I'll shoot you."

Byungwook laughed. It was a laugh that was hard to imagine coming from a man with numerous guns aimed at him. "Lower your gun, Captain Yeonsu. I'll explain everything."

"Soldiers, stand by to fire." At Yeonsu's words, the Hounds loaded their ammunition.

Byungwook grimaced. Yeonsu's gun began to waver, pointing at his forehead.

"You should be careful what your last words are, Captain," spat Yeonsu.

Byungwook clenched his jaw.

Just then, the *Okayama*'s dock released, and a small battleship could be heard setting off. Momentarily startled by the sound, Yeonsu's eyes filled with rage.

"You bastard! You were stalling for the Raven to escape?"

Byungwook grinned.

"Fire," Yeonsu ordered his men.

The rifles of the Hound Dog Squadron and the gunmen of the *Okayama* fired at the same time.

Yeonsu's stomach jolted as the Hounds' bullets stopped in mid-air. He took in Byungwook's smug expression. *Is there a Gifted among them?* Yeonsu wondered. *Guess he wasn't completely defenseless after all.*

Yeonsu smiled bitterly.

Another round of the Hounds' bullets flew at Byung-wook and his crew. Their bodies collapsed. The bullets fired by the *Okayama*'s crew hit the ground instead of their enemy.

Byungwook was slumped on the floor, spouting blood from his mouth. He must have been shot in the lungs. There was no hope. Yeonsu knelt down and took in Byungwook's trembling body.

"You people always believe that the Gifted are only on your side."

By the time Yeonsu stood up, Byungwook was lying dead in a puddle of blood.

"Good job, Danny," said Yeonsu.

His nephew, Danny Carlos, answered from behind him, "Yes, Captain."

Yeonsu slung his rifle onto his back and turned around to face the Hounds again.

"Return to the ship and track down the battleship."

Little Boy's hull began to recede. After a brief pause, the triangular hull propelled forward in the opposite direction of the *Okayama*, toward a small battleship that was now no bigger than a dot in the distance.

Yeonsu stared at the tail of the battleship from the cockpit.

"Lu Xun, increase the speed."

"This is the maximum output, Captain."

Yeonsu clicked his tongue. "They can't run forever. Ready the Gauss cannons."

The lower gunport opened, revealing a line of several gun barrels. When Aiden gave the signal, Yeonsu nodded. He looked toward the battleship again.

Raven, if I can't catch you, I'll kill you instead, he thought.

A humming noise started, and lasted for a few seconds. "Fire."

A ring of glowing fire stretched forward from *Little Boy*'s artillery. The battleship attempted an evasive maneuver to the right.

The ring had missed.

After completing the evasive maneuver, the battleship turned to the right of the *Little Boy* and started going straight.

If the ring had even slightly touched the battleship, it would have been destroyed. Regret and anger filled Yeonsu's bones. He gave another order.

"Recharge power. Cruise twenty degrees starboard."

Little Boy moved along the new path of the battleship.

We have them, Yeonsu thought. He was the commander of the front-line combat unit of the assault force, and he also led a squadron of five assault ships and a cruiser.

Raven, I see your flying skills. But there is no next time.

Yeonsu ordered the Hounds to calculate the White Raven's evasion direction and angle. He was driving the battleship within the coordinates of the *Little Boy*'s fire control system, where he wanted it.

The enemy battleship flew into the anticipated location. They were out of range in the control system. However, Yeonsu was sure that these coordinates would bring about the destruction of the battleship.

A humming sound filled the air.

Yeonsu jumped up from his seat and shouted, "Fire!"

The magnetic field surrounding the railgun had reached its peak.

A huge ship appeared in front of *Little Boy* and the battleship.

Lu Xun's blurted out, "What the hell is that?"

Yeonsu cried, "Stop the engine! Stop the engine! Maximize the front output! Damn it. Get your heads screwed on straight. Maximize the frontal RPM!"

The *Little Boy* staggered and rushed to withdraw the rear engine. The left engine had remained active, leaving the *Little Boy* to spin twice in its spot. Before long, the ship stood still.

A deeply perplexing atmosphere settled over the cockpit. Aiden was clutching his head where he'd banged it on the communication device as the ship made the sharp turn. His crewmates and captain were barely able to lift themselves up as they peered through the tempered glass at the ship floating in space before them. An oval body of enormous length and numerous guns.

A demonic symbol was engraved on the side engine and upper deck of the hull.

Lu Xun started with difficulty, "If I'm correct, we are looking at the *Robespierre*, Captain."

"I know, Lu Xun." Yeonsu's voice shook. This couldn't be happening.

The gigantic ship before their eyes was the cause of years of torment for the Desirée Union administration and the Planetary Alliance Command.

The Discarded Resistance mothership.

The last flagship.

The devil, *Robespierre*.

How did it appear so suddenly? thought Yeonsu angrily. *This is goes against all laws of physics.*

Yet, he knew this had happened before. The *Robespierre* was trouble for the Alliance's fleet because of its powerful firepower and durability, in addition to its puzzling maneuvering ability. The enemy ship always appeared out of nowhere, spewing fire from behind. No fleet in the Alliance could stop it. The number of cruisers and destroyers that had been shot down by this silent, demon-like ship alone had exceeded single digits a long time ago.

Its long and oval, dark gray hull and the armaments decorating the mast and both wings radiated an oppressive sense of intimidation. There was no other ship like this one in the entire Desirée star system.

Now, it was Yeonsu and his crew's turn to worry for their lives.

The dock bay of the *Robespierre* opened, and the battleship began to fly in their direction. Yeonsu racked his brain. What should he do? What was the right move? If they missed this opportunity to attack the ship, it could be a very long time until another opportunity would arise again. But he wasn't sure it was worth risking their lives, knowing how many had tried and failed before.

Yeonsu came to a decision. " Avoid all engagement with the *Robespierre* and retreat at full speed. Destination is Alpha, in the Shennong planetary system. Receive the Alpha's real-time coordinates. Lu Xun, put the engine output to the max."

Lu Xun nodded.

Little Boy turned its hull and began departing at full power.

The crewmembers, including Yeonsu, anxiously watched the movement of the *Robespierre*, a red dot on their three-dimensional radar map.

The *Robespierre* did not move.

"I don't think we're destined to die just yet, Captain," said Lu Xun, sounding relieved.

Yeonsu could read from the faces of Aiden, Kirox, Danny, and the other crewmembers that they were all thinking the same thing.

The *Robespierre* had no intention of attacking them.

But why? Was their goal merely to save the Raven?

Yeonsu had a bitter expression on his face. He muttered to himself, "See you again, Raven."

2.

After landing safely at the dock of the *Robespierre* and lifting its cover, the Raven climbed off the ship. A tall, white-haired man stood waiting to meet her.

"It's been a while, Cassie. Are you hurt?"

Cassie grabbed his outstretched hand and stood up. "I never thought the Hounds would search this far for us, Kamura."

Kamura Park, the shooting instructor and land battle commander for the Resistance, frowned. "We didn't either. It's unfortunate that the identity of the *Okayama* has been exposed. We're searching to find out how the information leaked as we speak."

"It's fine. There's no need for that. It's clear there was a spy. We'll have to be more careful when recruiting members in the future. Spies can be anywhere. Even in the Dark Zone."

Kamura shook his head. "They're getting clever. I understand. I'll pass it on to the scouts."

Cassie took off the white hood covering her head. "Where's Captain Joshua?"

"He's waiting for you on the bridge."

Cassie thanked Kamura and walked over to the bridge. Kamura's crew greeted her on the way.

"Cassie, you're still alive!" said *Robespierre*'s engineer, Redhead Miyabe. An older man greeted her with a hand signal by moving his arm and clenched fists up and down. Cassie responded with the same movements. Next was Kyungsu, an engineer from the Mining Guild.

Cassie walked past the crew lounge area and bar. Fighter pilots were gathered playing card games. Alpha Squadron's leader, Mei Yang, was sleeping with her feet propped up on a chair. She was known as one of the best pilots in the Resistance. Cassie was familiar with some of the *Robespierre*'s crewmembers, and others she only knew by face. There were also some she had never seen before.

Many of them were the survivors of the Big Crush.

When Cassie arrived at the bridge, Joshua Kwon was busy conversing with a number of people—operations officers, control officers, and flight commanders. When they saw Cassie, they each said hello. She nodded back and waited.

Joshua turned to her. "Cassie! I'm glad you're safe."

Cassie smiled. "I was surprised you didn't come greet me, Joshua."

"Ah, I've been a little busy. Shall we finish the meeting here?" he said to the others. "If there's anything left to discuss, I will contact you individually."

The *Robespierre* officers, who had been looking over a 3D star system map, nodded and returned to their positions one by one. Joshua led Cassie to his office.

Inside the captain's quarters, they sat down on the sofa. On the table near them, a small frame displayed a photograph of Joshua and Cassie, along with a young, dark-haired girl who looked to be about nine years old.

"Where's Yuna?" Cassie asked.

"I sent her to get some sleep. She's not used to life on a ship yet. Fortunately, there are children of the same age to keep her occupied. Some of the adults agreed to take turns teaching and looking after them."

Cassie thought of her daughter, Yuna, and how much she'd missed her. Joshua looked at Cassie deep in thought and called to her in a soft voice.

"Cassie."

"Yeah?"

"I'm glad you're back. I was really worried."

Cassie looked to Joshua and laughed. "Were you scared that I might die?"

"If anything happened to you, I would have broken into the Alliance headquarters. I wouldn't have let them get away with it."

"That would be committing suicide, you know that, right? At least, I hope you know it."

"I'd rather be dead than alive in a world without you."

Cassie shook her head. "You have Yuna. Whatever happens to me, you have to take care of Yuna first. No matter what."

Joshua looked at Cassie with a sad expression. He suddenly remembered the beer inside the mini fridge in the closet and pulled it out. He poured it into a glass and handed it to Cassie, who smiled in thanks.

"A lifesaver," she said.

The beer was prickly and cold running down her throat.

Cassie savored the beer a little more with her tongue, and then asked, "What about the *Okayama*?"

"We've sent a collection squadron. They'll clean up the situation and bring the ship back to normal. If things get worse, they'll rescue the remaining crew and bring them back."

"That's good."

"I don't feel good about it. I feel like I've been punched in the face by those punks from the Alliance."

Cassie understood what he meant. The *Okayama* had been on a mission to raid an orbital colony in the Desirée star system. In addition, since Discarded's infamous hacker and fighter White Raven had been aboard the aircraft, the Resistance had undoubtedly had high expectations for the *Okayama*'s performance.

"Did you see who raided *Okayama*?" asked Joshua.

"No, but Captain Byungwook did. He called them the Hounds."

"The Hound Dog Squadron?" His eyes narrowed. "So, it was them."

"You know who they are?"

Joshua clenched his teeth. "The Alliance Hounds. They're a special forces squadron in charge of spying, counterintelligence, assassination, and raid operations. We've lost quite a few members to them. You were lucky to get away from them, Cassie."

"We should have pursued them and eradicated them."

"It would've been too dangerous. I didn't want you involved in it. Besides, the ship's maintenance hasn't been completed yet, so the battle weapons aren't ready yet. We have to conserve resources as much as possible—not engage in an operation that could damage them further."

Cassie looked toward Han, the burning planet and the motherland of the old Mining Guild.

A memory flashed in her mind of the day when a blinding white light swept through the sky. When thousands of lives lost in the clouds poured down toward the ground. The countless moments in the cold and frozen Dark Zone after Cassie learned the truth about what had happened, when she vowed to return those deaths to the Alliance.

Joshua's voice pulled her from her thoughts of the past.

"Karl Ryoma contacted us. He asked to meet."

Cassie's brows lifted in surprised. "You're in touch with the Root Restorationists?"

Joshua nodded. "They have supporters among us too, right?"

Cassie remembered the engineer, Kyungsu, who greeted her by waving his arm up and down, in the same motion as someone planting roots. Such a movement meant that Kyungsu was a supporter of the Root Restoration Sect. Members of the sect believed in searching for their roots in the earth and early species, and one day returning to them. They claimed that everything in the migrant star system far from their home was flawed.

All human beings who settled in the Desirée star system had arrived there in one of the four large-scale migration ships that appeared in the system around 370 years ago. The four ships were called *Fuxi*, *Amaterasu*, *Hwanung*, and *James Cook*. The ships each found their way to three different planetary systems within the Desirée. The people aboard *Hwanung* settled on Han, a rocky planet in the Haemosu planetary system, and later formed the Mining Guild. Other travelers made their home on the planet Amaterasu, in the same system, named after the ship that settled there. *James Cook* and *Fuxi* each settled on New Sydney and New Shanghai of the Behemoth and Shennong planetary systems, respectively, and became the birthplace of the Planetary Alliance.

Hundreds of years had passed since humans settled in the Desirée system, and generations of descendants, not immigrants, had been born who lived not knowing or remembering anything of their homeland other than the information on various media records.

As the leader and founder "sage" Karl Ryoma claimed, the Restorationists denied the "Brave New World" they were born in, and insisted humans needed to return to Earth, the home and motherland of all mankind, a place they did not remember and thus longed for even more. The Alliance soon began to keep a close eye on them. Although it had not yet been recognized as a rebellious force and cracked down on a large scale, the Restoration group was a potential threat to the unity of the Alliance.

Cassie got up and walked over to Joshua and stroked his cheek. Joshua closed his eyes.

"Joshua. Can those people…be of strength to us? Those who believe we should return to our origins? Those who call us to flee without resisting against the tyranny of the Alliance? I know that you, more than anyone else, understand to the core everything that the Alliance has done."

In his mind, Joshua saw an image of his late wife, Jiyeon, covered in blood.

On the day of the Big Crush, he had been in a hurry to get out of the air base in New Seongnam, on the planet Han, to find her and his daughter, Amy. Instead, he found his house in ruins, thanks to the missiles fired by an unidentified aircraft in the sky.

Joshua couldn't find Amy, but he stumbled upon Jiyeon's body as she lay dying among the rubble. He wanted desperately to save her, but the damaged structure was on the verge of total collapse. Jiyeon said something to him, but all Joshua heard was a hissing sound. A steel frame had penetrated her neck. The foam of blood dribbled from her mouth.

The building collapsed, burying her body, and the hissing ceased.

Now, Joshua pictured Jiyeon smiling. The scene came to his mind from time to time. It would appear to him suddenly at random times and places, and continued to torment him. The days when Amy would cling to him and smile while they made brunch together. Memories of the three of them on a picnic. Memories of them fighting, laughing, chatting and hugging each other.

Moments he would never live again.

"We need to grow stronger, Cassie." Joshua spoke in a hoarse voice. He opened his eyes and took Cassie's hand. "If someone has the power to help us, we should use it. Whoever they are. If their power can protect us and destroy our enemies in any way."

Cassie looked at him silently and kissed him.

When Cassie entered the cabin, Yuna was asleep. Cassie carefully undressed and changed into more casual clothes. As she finished pulling on her shirt, her daughter called to her.

"Mom!"

Cassie looked at her daughter, pretending to be startled. The girl smiled and jumped up to hug her mother. Mother and daughter fell to the bed. For a short moment, they rolled around, entangled together. Yuna giggled with delight. Cassie made a choking sound as Yuna tickled her.

After a while, the two lay still, exhausted, catching their breath. Cassie ran her hand through Yuna's short, dark hair.

"My puppy, why weren't you asleep?"

"I slept a lot earlier. I was waiting for you. Why did you take so long? It feels like it's been days since I've seen you." Yuna pouted.

"I'm sorry. I was working. How was it today? Did you study?"

"I studied history. Redhead Miyabe was the teacher for today. My friends and I learned a lot about the First Name War. It was really strange that there was a war over what name people should use. And for a long time, too."

Cassie chuckled. "People are like that. They argue over nothing and blame each other for it. You know that our ancestors were all migrants, right? We were people from all different cultures and environments. That's where this kind of hatred started, even before we got here."

"Yeah, but that was a long time ago."

"That's right. The First Name War was a foolish war that started with a spark that arrived in this world 400 years ago. But Yuna, the war was never about names. Inheriting a name is something that everyone is born with. It's an inherent right."

"Inher…" Yuna scrunched her mouth. "What does that mean?"

"Gosh, I guess I used a difficult word. It means that everyone was born with this right. Our ancestors were all like that. Earthlings inherited their parents' surnames. Most cultures were like that. But here it's different, right?

Because a computer randomly assigns the child's last name. It is no longer possible to know who is whose child by their name alone. That means people are not recognized as people. We've erased all individuality, severing history. The First Name War…well, it was a war waged by egotistical people who wished to oppress others and would not recognize them as human beings."

Karl Ryoma could possibly ignite the Third Name War, Cassie thought to herself. At the end of the First Name War, the Planetary Alliance and the Mining Guild had abolished social and political restrictions on names of different cultures within their territory. When a child was born, they were given a surname generated by the government's lottery system. The random surname system sparked the Second Name War more than a decade later. It was a never-ending conflict.

With the incorporation of the planets Han and Valhalla into the Alliance twenty and ten years ago, respectively, random surnames became the fate of most humans in the Desirée system, save for a select few.

Are we better off than the people of Valhalla who are not even given a surname? Cassie held back a scoff.

"Yuna," she continued. "We are all descendants of migrants, so we don't want to lose our roots and heritage. The Alliance believes that identity and individuality ultimately lead to the forming of groups and conflict. That's the silly reason behind the war."

Perhaps it was because humans were not meant to be lonely and independent beings. The two Name Wars had come and gone. Now, fifty years later, the sparks of conflict from the past had shifted into a movement of restoration.

"Who gave me my name?" asked Yuna.

"Huh?"

"My name is different from yours. I heard that my name is from East Asia on the original planet. But my surname is Ice, and your name is Anglo-Saxon. That's why I was wondering if my dad gave me this name and not you. Is that right, Mom?"

Cassie was startled. She looked to Yuna for a brief moment. The child grew bigger by day. This little human had grown up and become quite perplexing.

"That's right, baby. Your name was given to you by your biological father. I guess you can say he's your real father." Cassie laughed. But her eyes looked somewhat sad.

"The person you got separated from during the Big Crush?" asked Yuna.

Cassie stood up. "That's right." She reached for the light switch and turned it off. "I'll tell you about that later. Mommy is tired today."

3.

New Shanghai was the motherland of the Planetary Alliance and was located in the Shennong planetary system, within the Desirée. The Alliance Defense Command was based in New Shanghai. It was one of the four habitable planets on which travelers from the migrant ship *Fuxi* had settled, and it was a warm, temperate planet home to many Alliance research centers, after numerous development and advancements. The capital city was called Altra, named after the company that had long ago invested a massive amount of money into the *Fuxi* and led the establishment of the planet when the ship first landed, before later ceasing operations.

New Shanghai was also the main stage for the secret special forces led by Captain Yeonsu. He returned to the planet exactly three days after the attack on the *Okayama*. As soon as he submitted his report to Command, Yeonsu headed to his apartment. Exhaustion dug deep into his bones.

When he got out of the shower, Yeonsu saw a message from Harry Carlos on his phone. Yeonsu clicked on his name. Moments later, a hologram of Harry appeared.

"I'm back, Harry," said Yeonsu.

"How's Danny?" asked Harry.

"He did his part this time; he stopped the enemy bullets with telekinesis. There was a telekinetic among the Resistance, but he couldn't overpower Danny. He's probably resting right now."

"I heard the Raven got away."

Yeonsu nodded, rubbing his forehead. "We ran into the *Robespierre*. I considered going after it anyway, but from the moment that monster-like ship appeared, it was already decided."

"I'm not saying it's your fault. However, it's a shame."

"Is there anything I should know from Command?"

"We can't understand what the Discarded are after. They attack sporadically, but lately they've been quiet. Command's getting nervous about it. They don't like that we have no insight into their plan. "Any news from the spy?"

"I don't know. Joshua Kwon seems to be up to something, but it's all top secret. No one around him knows his intentions."

Yeonsu considered for a moment. "Harry, I met Commander Byungwook on the *Okayama*."

Harry narrowed his eyes. "So, he's become a traitor. Have you dealt with him?"

"Yes, but he said something I didn't understand."

"And what was that?"

"He said the Alliance was behind the Big Crush. What does that mean? Do you have any idea, Harry?"

Harry blinked a few times let out a cynical laugh. "It's

nonsense. A conspiracy with no evidence. I've heard that their captains enchant people with such stories. I didn't know former Commander Byungwook would take part in it as well, that knave."

Yeonsu did not respond. His thoughts were consumed by Byungwook's words and expression as he was faced with death.

And then the sudden appearance of the *Robespierre*.

"The *Robespierre* was carrying top-secret Alliance technology, Harry."

"What do you mean?"

"It's like I said; their flagship appeared out of nowhere. Isn't that a recently developed technology known only to a handful of people at the Alliance Research Institute? For a flagship to materialize like that…it must be carrying our technology. That's the only explanation." Yeonsu tried to recall the term. "Warp drive technology. It has to be a wormhole generator."

Harry's brow creased. "You're sure?"

"Yes. I saw it myself. If I'm correct, it makes sense why other Alliance ships have been attacked unexpectedly before they could counterattack. But how did they get their hands on the technology? Could there be a spy in the Alliance Research Institute, Harry?"

"Maybe so…" Harry looked deep in thought. "Discuss it with your superiors, seriously. I need to get some sleep now."

Yeonsu yawned before he could answer.

Harry chuckled. "Actually, you should get to bed. You must be tired," said his hologram. "I'll fill in Command and let them know what you said, so don't worry about it."

"Thank you, Father."

Harry's hologram disappeared.

Yeonsu took a beer out of the refrigerator and sat down on the small sofa. He bobbed his leg and took a sip of the beer, thinking again of the *Robespierre*.

He had seen ships appearing as if by teleportation like that one other time. On that day twenty years ago, when the sky above planet Han was filled with blinding light.

The ships had been carrying the Eaters. Those ships had filled the sky that day, before anyone in the Mining Guild noticed. As the ships poured toward the ground, they bombarded buildings and people with photon plasma and missiles.

Yeonsu's eyelids trembled.

The Eaters had appeared after the supernova explosion. When the devastation of the Mining Guild was complete, an Alliance spokesman gave a speech about the incident. He said that the Alliance had driven out the Eaters, and they were in the process of identifying the individuals behind the attack. That as long as the Alliance handled matters from now on, these people would never appear again.

Yeonsu still didn't believe a word of it. Watching the Eaters' aircraft flying through the sky, young Yeonsu had known that their technology far exceeded anything in their star system.

If Commander Harry Carlos's contingent had not discovered him and saved him from the devastation, Yeonsu would not be alive today.

Burning cities. Collapsing buildings and debris. The screams of people as they ran away.

A loud noise wrenched Yeonsu from his memories. He looked down to see the beer can was crushed in his grasp.

Yeonsu stared at the crushed can for a while and then threw it into the sink.

4.

Karl Ryoma asked to meet in the nearby asteroid zone. He said he would cross over to the *Robespierre* himself.

When Cassie first laid eyes on Karl Ryoma, she was reminded of a panda, a creature from Earth she had seen once in New Shanghai. Karl was a big and tall black man. He came into the captain's room, led by Kamura, who promptly left.

"Nice to meet you," said Karl, offering his large hand to Joshau. "I'm Karl Ryoma."

Joshua shook his hand. "I'm Joshua Kwon of the Discarded."

"And who is this?" Karl's eyes shifted to Cassie, who gave him a nod.

"This is a fellow comrade, White Raven," said Joshua. "Have you heard the name?

His eyes widened a bit. "Ah. Resistance ravens are famous within the star system. A year ago, I never would've thought I'd meet you like this."

"Likewise," said Joshua. "You've amassed a great number of believers these days, including among my crew."

"I'm grateful to the friends who acknowledge my goal. But they are not believers, as I have not created a religion," said Karl with a chuckle. "I just let others know that there are other ways for the people of the Desirée to advance forward, and I provide help to those in need."

"Some people call such a person a prophet."

At Cassie's words, Karl Ryoma frowned slightly. "Call me Karl. I'm no prophet, even if some people feel that way about me."

Joshua grinned. "Whatever you are, I hope you can help us too."

"Of course, I'll do what I can."

Karl Ryoma glanced around the captain's room. Cassie watched him silently. For the head of the mysterious Root Restorationists, he was a rather friendly and selfless man.

"So, this is *Robespierre*, the nightmare of the Alliance Fleet," he said. "Tell me, who's behind your ship? Is it the Diutinians?"

Joshua raised his brows, and Cassie's mouth fell open in shock. Karl let out a laugh.

"You know about them, Karl?" asked Joshua.

"But how did you find out?" Cassie blurted out.

"There's no need to be startled. To get your hands on a wormhole generator in this star system, there are only two possibilities." Karl met Joshua's eyes. "It's either from the ruins of the mines, or alien technology."

"You're a learned man," said Joshua. "For your information, we are calling the wormhole generator the pathfinding module. As you said, it's not of the Mining Guild. It's alien."

"I see. This may be out of place, but do you have a cold drink?" asked Karl.

"Would you like some beer? That's how I quench my thirst."

"Beer sounds excellent."

Cassie poured two beers from Joshua's fridge into glasses and handed one each to Joshua and Karl.

"None for you, Lady Raven?" asked Karl.

"I'm all right."

"Let's drink together. Please."

Cassie looked to Joshua, who nodded, so she filled a third cup for herself before sitting down again.

"Honestly, I was surprised. I didn't think you would figure it out right away." Joshua started.

"It was a hunch," said Karl, taking a sip of his beer. "The Big Crush incident surprised many people in many ways. I used to work as a trader and an interpreter in the past. Among the merchants who traveled between star systems, I often heard legends of unidentified aliens that would appear deep in outer space, and the mysterious devices they would bring. The energy those devices unleashed was incredible. It's an open secret that the Alliance has been desperate to get their hands on alien technology. So, is it really the Diutinians behind you?"

"Yes, but not the entire Diutin community. Only a small portion are helping us."

"That's real surprising news." Karl clicked his tongue. He gulped down the rest of his beer in one breath.

Cassie watched him closely, wondering what scheme he was up to. "Karl, I want to know what your thoughts were when you contacted us," she said after a moment. "Are you also against the Planetary Alliance, or at least their actions and philosophies? If so, are you planning to join us in our fight against the Alliance?"

Karl looked at Cassie with an unreadable expression. "The Alliance is powerful, Lady Raven."

"It's Cassie. And I know they're strong, Karl. We've been fighting against the mighty Alliance for a long time now. I'm sure you know that."

"Cassie. I am well aware of the espionage, secret operations, and acts of terror you have carried out against the Alliance. And I have heard of the work of the *Robespierre* and other Resistance fighters. But war is another matter. What your people are doing is terrorism, not war. Are you planning to go head to head with the Alliance? If so, I have to say it's a hopeless move."

"Then why did you contact us?" Joshua said with his arms crossed.

Karl's dark eyes turned to him. The two looked at each other.

After a while, Karl laughed and Joshua followed.

"Because I need it too," said Karl.

"What do you mean?"

Karl pointed to the floor. "A ship with a warp drive."

"We cannot give you our ship."

Karl smiled and winked at Joshua. "Do I look like a thief? Who comes to ask for a boat? I don't want the *Robespierre*."

"Then where are you looking for such a ship?"

"In the secret dock of the Alliance."

"You mean the Alliance has such a ship?" Cassie cut in.

"Yes. And I'm going to steal it."

Joshua's eyes narrowed with suspicion. "You don't mean…?"

"I'm taking my comrades to Mother Earth," said Karl firmly. "Do you know about the Lightspeed Outer Space Exploration Project?"

Cassie's eyes lit up at Karl Ryoma's words. Joshua put a hand on her shoulder.

Karl nodded as he saw their reactions. "I guess you do."

Cassie scoffed, but her eyes didn't smile. "Of course, I do. I participated in it myself."

"Did you? Were you a volunteer?"

"I was."

"Where did you go?"

"Seven light-years away to Alpha Genesis."

Karl gave her a sympathetic look. "You have seen many things, then.

"Many of our crews were volunteers and scapegoats for that project, Karl." Joshua spoke in a calm voice. "The Alliance was particularly keen on promoting the project to refugees from the Mining Guild. It was a perfect way for them to deal with the 'troublesome' refugees."

Cassie thought about her past. The hellish days when she went through hell and back for Yuna. All the kinds of illegal dealings she'd experienced between the planets Han, New Shanghai, New Sydney, and her home planet that had become a living hell. Horrible days of smuggling newly developed drugs and having to assassinate complete strangers.

One day, an elderly man who identified himself as an agent of the Alliance had come to see her. He told Cassie that if she participated in the Alliance's Outer Space Exploration Project and pioneered an unidentified area, she would receive in return compensation that was incomparable to what she had previously been offered. In addition, if she were to develop a colony on a planet that she pioneered, she would receive additional payment depending on the degree of development. The man whispered all of this in a voice as slippery as a snake.

Cassie made several short voyages with Yuna, and the man paid a hefty pay each time. Each time she returned to the system, she noticed that time in this star system was running a little faster than her own. But Cassie couldn't stop.

When they arrived at the last coordinates she was given, Alpha Genesis, Cassie was greeted by the Dark Zone. There, she saw the remains of dead planets, interstellar gas, and the graves of ships that had lost fuel and become a part of the landscape. The Alliance was constantly developing engine technology capable of outer space navigation, and it needed continuous tests. The Alliance had sent refugees from the Mining Guild, including Cassie, on beaten-down ships with only a change of engine, to set sail on hopeless explorations with coordinates where they would meet their death. It wasn't the Alpha that Cassie met in the Dark Zone but the Omega.

Cassie felt an endless fear in that darkness. Around the time she landed, the ship carrying Cassie had exhausted all its fuel. The ship automatically transmitted their flight data to Alliance Command, seven light-years away. That was the ship's last exploration.

An interstellar gas storm enveloped the ship, and the resulting light assaulted the ship. Huddled together in the endless darkness, where no light from the stars could reach them, Cassie and Yuna prepared for death.

As she sobbed in the depths of the universe, she saw a man. The man she loved. The man who had disappeared from her life amongst the dizzying lights of the Big Crush. The man who had gifted her with Yuna.

Cassie saw the man approaching them and thought, *So, this is what death is like.* It was a painless and instantaneous death. *You've been waiting for me this whole time.*

Cassie smiled.

"Are you okay?" asked the man.

Hearing his voice, Cassie came to her senses. This was a different man. Someone new.

The man looked to her and gave instructions to those who were with him. Before long, they helped her and her daughter out of the collapsing ship.

The man was Joshua Kwon, and he would become Cassie's second everything.

She had fallen deep into herself when Karl's voice brought her back to the surface.

"The Lightspeed Outer Space Exploration Project. It's a project that the Alliance has been planning for a long time," he was saying.

Joshua looked completely unprepared for his words.

"That ship is said to be equipped with a wormhole generator, much like the one the Diutins provided for *Robespierre*," continued Karl. "I don't know if it's the same technology, but according to my sources, it should work, whether as standalone or not."

Joshua weighed his words. "Is that what you're asking us to help you with? To capture this ship?"

"Yes, Captain."

"Why us? Why haven't you done it yourself, Karl?"

Karl laughed, not seeming at all startled by Joshua's direct questioning. "We have far bigger numbers than you, but very few agents capable of guerrilla warfare or counterintelligence. In that field, you're the experts."

"And what do we gain from this operation?"

Karl glared at Joshua. Cassie felt a burning desire and anger coming from his eyes. An anger that Karl had been hiding from them until now, allowing it to brew and intensify.

"An alliance with the Root Restorationists, new technology, and…"

"And?"

"The uprising of all the Restorationists in the system." Karl reached out to Joshua. "We're going to write a new history for humanity."

Joshua glanced at Cassie. A number of dizzying thoughts swirled around her head. An armed uprising, a war, ships equipped with wormhole generators, and a return to Earth… All these entangled thoughts led to a single conclusion.

The collapse of the Planetary Alliance.

But is it possible? she wondered.

Joshua took Karl's hand. "Let's do it."

5.

Altra's sky was always full of ships leaping into space and entering the docks of the planet. About 60 percent of the population of the Desirée star system lived in New Shanghai, and Altra was a large city home to about 20 percent of New Shanghai's residents. The city's harbors and docks were always crowded with spaceships and land ships. Although the First and Second Name Wars had left much civil disturbance and riots in several planets in the system, Altra had never been exposed to such rebellious intentions. This was through the enormous efforts of the Alliance government to defend New Shanghai and Altra. As a result, the Alliance Research Institute had naturally been established in the eastern outskirts of Altra, the safest place in the system.

Yeonsu revealed his military personnel card to the guards at the institute. The guard nodded and opened the door to the lab. Yeonsu had come to meet Danny for lunch. The guards led him to Sector B, where the Gifted of the

Alliance Command were training.

Unlike the many laboratories of Sector A filled with researchers in gowns, Sector B was occupied by Allied soldiers clad in dark gray and black clothes. Yeonsu greeted the soldiers he was acquainted with. The guard led him farther into the sector, until they came to a dark, isolated room beyond a bulkhead.

Danny stood alone inside the room, wearing protective gear and surrounded by various objects and holograms. Upon seeing him through the transparent wall, Yeonsu's brow creased.

"What kind of training is this?"

The trainer, also watching through the transparent wall, turned to look at him. "It's for his reflects, to help him practice knowing the right time and place to use telekinesis. He has to move those objects to the area displayed on the screen. If he's even a little late, he'll lose points. At five points, it's a failed challenge."

Upon closer inspection, Yeonsu saw a screen at the top of the dark room's opposite wall. As "A-3" was displayed on the screen, Danny floated one of the objects of unknown material into the air and moved it to a corner. As "C-14" appeared, another object flew around Danny. At D-1 and F-1, objects were created opposite each other, and then two of them swapped positions.

The highlight was seeing Danny gather a group of objects all created at the same time in five different places and burn them. The trainer applauded.

After a while, Danny came out of the dark room drenched in sweat to see Yeonsu.

"Captain."

"Call me Uncle. I'm off duty today."

Danny laughed. "I thought you would be a hermit in your room."

"I tried to do that, but I couldn't last a week. Let's go get a meal in the city. It's been a while."

"Give me a minute to change clothes."

"Sure. Did you bring the A-wing?"

"It's in the back hangar."

"Good. I'll wait at the entrance. See you in a little bit."

Yeonsu had been waiting at the entrance of the Research Institute for a moment when he heard the sound of a plasma motor engine unique to the A-wing. Soon, Danny's A-wing, an old two-seater model, appeared in the air. The A-shaped shell served as an axle, and maintained a sense of balance when moving in the air. As an individual means of transportation for most of the residents of the star system, its origins were the spherical mobiles of old Earth. As far as Yeoonsu knew, Danny's A-wing was almost eight years old, but its maneuvering was still solid. As the A-wing landed, the right cover opened, revealing Danny.

"Get in, Uncle."

Once Yeonsu got on board and leaned back into the seat, the cover closed with a mechanical sound.

"Shall we go for it?"

Danny entered the destination into the dashboard. Soon, the travel time appeared on the instrument panel, along with a message indicating the automatic driving system was activated. Thirty minutes.

The A-wing's plasma motor blew out fire. Soon after, the ship took off and began to follow the flight path while increasing acceleration.

Within a moment, the A-wing flew into Jiangwei

Bridge, west of downtown Altra. The twenty kilometer-long bridge was still functioning as a link between Altra and its surrounding cities 200 years after its construction. Just 200 years ago, vehicles with wheels drove on this bridge, but today, it was only A-wings coming and going through the cylindrical aerial vehicle passages that connected the two ends of the bridge. All other airspaces were designated as illegal airspace under the Alliance Constitution. This was an attempt by the Alliance to prevent noise and visual pollution caused by the aerial vehicles from bothering residents.

Danny's A-wing flew through the bridge for another ten minutes before landing in the parking sector of a restaurant. As they turned off the engine and got out of the vehicle, Yeonsu realized where they were—The Guesthouse.

"Is this place popular these days?"

"Of course. Try the lamb ribs, Uncle. They're super clean and have no odor."

As they entered the place, elegantly dressed ladies appeared to greet them. Danny smiled and asked for a window seat.

Soon they were led to a room by the window, behind a sliding door. The window offered a view of the Jiangwei Bridge and the city. Danny ordered four servings of lamb ribs along with appetizers and drinks, and after about twenty minutes, the table was set with meat, soup, and vegetables.

Yeonsu put on a mean expression. "Tell me honestly, nephew, why you brought me here. Do you have a lover here?"

Danny looked at Yeonsu with a startled face. "What? Why would you bring that up all of a sudden?"

"It's okay. I didn't tell your grandfather. But don't try to fool me. You didn't think I know that you're always on the phone after training?"

"I swear you're wrong, Uncle. That's a really surprising insight, but you're barking up the wrong tree, I'm sorry to say."

"Should I ask your colleagues if it really is the wrong tree?"

Danny's expression was now beyond bewildered. "Who told you?"

"Well, someone close to you, I guess."

Danny's eyes narrowed and he muttered, "Aiden, that unscrupulous bastard."

"Now, don't be too harsh on your colleague," said Yeonsu, reaching for his drink to take a sip. "Aiden did not want to give up your secret. He only told me under the premise that another member of the unit would go to training for the winter dispatch in his place."

"So, he sold off my love life for a training exemption? That still makes him a bastard," said Danny, staring angrily at the meat on his plate.

The door slowly opened, and a slim, short-haired woman appeared with a serving cart. She smiled as she looked at Danny.

"You're back again."

Danny's demeanour shifted in an instant from angry to smiling mischievously. Yeonsu clicked his tongue. This woman had to be Danny's lover.

When the woman had finished serving them, Yeonsu spoke up, "So, how long have you been with Danny, miss? I'm not sure what to call you."

The woman's face flushed in embarrassment for a

moment, but then she answered with a smile, "I guess you made it quite obvious, Danny. What's your relationship with this keen person?"

Danny sighed. "This is my uncle, Yuri. He's only keen in times like these."

Yuri gracefully placed her hand on her chest and bowed slightly. "Nice to meet you, Lieutenant Colonel Carlos. I've heard about you from Danny. I'm Yuri Ivanova, the owner of The Guesthouse. My original name was Yurina, but now I go by Yuri. Please call me whatever you like."

Yeonsu laughed. He liked this woman. Looking at Danny's expression, Yeonsu understood what it was about Yuri that had captured his heart.

"You're an assertive hostess, I see. Although we have only just met, I like your character. Take care of Danny, please."

"I will. I'll leave you two to talk. Danny, see me before you leave. And drink in moderation."

After she left the room, Yeonsu chuckled at his nephew. "You look so stupid, Danny, no matter how much you like her. Can't you do something with that expression?"

Danny coughed. "Uncle, you're not going to tell Grandpa, right?"

"I won't. You know how intense that old man can get. I'd never hear the end of it. Let's eat."

Danny and Yeonsu started devouring the marinated grilled lamb as if they'd been starved. Their appetites dominated the table, creating peace for a while. Yeonsu was drinking strong liquor and became lost in thought. Danny noticed his uncle's expression and put down the bone he was holding in his hand.

"What's wrong?"

"Did you tell the hostess? That you're a Gifted?"

"I did. She didn't seem to care."

Yeonsu was amazed. Yuri was a bolder woman than he thought.

Select humans who had encountered the Eaters during the Big Crush had developed abilities that humans had never possessed before. The Alliance had later learned that this was a kind of telekinesis that allowed the Gifted to move objects or change their properties. Children with telekinesis were starting to be born to parents who had also acquired telekinesis. Danny was one of those children. Their descendants were also born with the same telekinetic powers as their fathers or mothers. However, most of these children came from poor backgrounds. The human body's inability to endure these powers resulted in these children becoming orphans. Such had been the case for Danny after he lost his father, Sean Carlos.

The Alliance marked people like Danny as Gifted, and issued a separate registration certificate. The intention was to raise them into elite psychokinesis agents—in other words, killing machines.

However, among them were many who could not withstand the self-destruction caused by the excessive mental exhaustion accompanying their abilities. About two years ago in the year 2912, eight years after the Alliance annexed the last remaining planet, Valhalla, in a small town in New Sydney, Connecticut, a man named Joe Milligan, called "Gloomy Joe," had massacred members of the Allied forces as well as citizens in a shopping mall with more than 1,000 people. It was an incident that no one could forget. An Allied elite or a mental breakdown—either extreme was the fate of the Gifted. And it was Danny who had stopped the tragedy that day. He was the hero of New Sydney, the savior of Connecticut. Danny didn't like to talk about the incident, though. Yeonsu was especially careful not to talk about it in front of Danny.

Danny had also gone through several episodes of near mental breakdown. Yeonsu remembered Harry's devastation upon seeing the two-year-old baby floating various objects in the air. Danny was a precious child. The last of Sean Carlos left in the world.

Yeonsu had practically raised Danny. They might not have been connected by blood, but Danny was still like a son to him.

Because of such reasons and events, the Gifted were a particularly taboo subject for the citizens of the Alliance. Naturally, people were hesitant to accept these people as sons-in-law or daughters-in-law, as they believed they carried dangerous abilities that could cause mental breakdowns and annihilate friends and family. It was a yoke that the Gifted would have to carry for the rest of their lives.

Yeonsu was relieved by Danny's bright expression. He also felt a great appreciation for the woman named Yuri. Yeonsu truly wished a happy life for Danny.

One day, Danny had asked Yeonsu why he didn't have a lover and why he wasn't married. Yeonsu explained to Danny that it was something he could not get involved with anymore. It was twenty years ago, on the day of the Big Crush, when Yeonsu realized this for the first time. Yeonsu wanted Danny to feel the happiness that ordinary people felt, unlike himself.

"Is the selection for the *Cheng Ho* Project finished, Uncle?"

Yeonsu realized after a moment that Danny was talking

about the Alliance government's superluminal expedition into outer space. Danny emptied his drink.

"It's almost complete," said Yeonsu.

"Are there any assigned soldiers?"

"I'm sure there are. People from all walks of life and jobs and backgrounds were up as candidates, so I'm sure the military will be included."

"Grandpa doesn't say a word to us about it."

Seeing Danny's disheartened expression, Yeonsu shook his head. "Don't be too disappointed, Danny. No one knows what the outcome of that project will be. It's full of dangers. A warp drive through a wormhole… God knows what they'll encounter in that star system. It's likely they'll see some really terrible things. Do you think Harry's going to let us be a part of that project?"

Danny let out a groan. He was running out of alcohol, so he ordered another drink. When a container of clear liquid arrived, Danny drank again. Yeonsu stopped his hand.

"Stop drinking, Danny. You're already tipsy."

Danny glanced at Yeonsu once and then at his wrist. "Okay, Uncle."

Yeonsu's shoulders relaxed a bit in relief. Danny was a good kid, but sometimes he showed a lack of restraint in his drinking. Perhaps the hostess's words played a part in his moderation.

"Why do you think they won't send a probe to Earth?"

Yeonsu looked at Danny. His nephew was looking down at the table, puzzled.

"What do you mean?" he asked.

"With such technology, it makes more sense to send it to the motherland of mankind first. Isn't it strange they aren't, Uncle?"

Yeonsu could not answer. Because he didn't know the answer either.

It had been nearly 400 years since humans had settled in the Desirée system. However, human and material exchanges could not be made between this system and Earth, the home of the original humans. There existed a 200-year space-time gap between Earth and the planetary systems of the Desirée, prohibiting all interaction. The first migrants aboard the fleet had arrived to this star system in hibernation to stop them from aging physically. Their ancestors who formed the early Planetary Alliance had received radio signals coming from Earth, signaling an obvious truth.

"Migration fleets, answer the call of the motherland."

The signal had come from Earth 200 years prior. In the end, even photon communication and radio waves could not overcome the limit of the speed of light.

The members of the migrant fleet spoke many native languages of the original human race. However, as time passed, its usage and pronunciations had grown varied. Many people were aware that the star system was actually called the Desire, but the name had been solidified by the president of New Shanghai, who was not familiar with English.

In this way, all timely exchange between the original human beings who had sowed the seeds of hope into the universe and the humans of the migrant fleet was cut off. Nonetheless, the Desirée Union administration had continued to send radio and photon signals back to Earth, in the hopes someone was receiving their communication back in the motherland, in a different time.

But then came the day when the delayed signals from Earth had stopped arriving, 100 years ago. On that day, the Desirée Alliance government had experienced a great crisis. They could not figure out what this all meant. Either the original humans of Earth were extinct, or they had forgotten all about the humans who left.

Perhaps the only remaining human life in this galaxy was the Alliance of the Desirée system. This was a frightening realization for humanity.

The Alliance government might have already given up on Earth, but that didn't mean every human had. Now, they had far more advanced navigational technology compared to when Earth had sent their ancestors into space 600 years ago. A warp drive navigation system enabling faster-than-light systems that could dilute space-time difference.

Yeonsu took hold of Danny's drink and poured it into his mouth before getting up.

"Where are you going?" asked Danny.

"Toilet. Let's leave when I get back." Yeonsu wanted to cool his head.

On his way back from the bathroom, Yeonsu noticed a man in the restaurant. He was a tall man with short, white hair, and something about his presence made him quite memorable. Yeonsu observed the man for a moment. Yuri walked up to the man and asked a few questions, and the man replied to her. Yeonsu couldn't hear their conversation from his distance, though, so eventually, he turned away from them and returned to his table. Danny stood up when Yeonsu walked into the room.

"Shall we go, Uncle?"

"Yes, let's head out." Yeonsu left the room, and Danny followed.

Yuri approached them in a hurry. "How was your meal?"

Yeonsu smiled. "It was very good. Please give the chef our compliments, Yuri."

"I will. I'm sure he'll be delighted to hear it." Yuri grabbed Danny's arm. He was smiling down at her as if mesmerized by her face. "Danny, wait. I want to speak with you."

Danny's smile fell a bit. Yeonsu gave them space and nodded to Danny. "Go. I'll wait for you."

Yuri led Danny to the corner of the hall.

"What's going on, Yuri?" he asked.

"I have something to tell you," she said in a rush.

"What is that?"

"Take care of yourself."

Danny grinned. "Are you worried? It's what I always do."

"No, you have to be especially careful today."

Danny was taken aback by Yuri's serious expression. All signs of laughter were erased from her face.

"I don't know what you'll think later, but…no matter what happens today, take care of yourself first. Okay?"

Danny nodded blankly. He was a little drunk, and he thought she was a little more emotional than usual. "Okay. Don't worry." He put a hand on her shoulder.

Yuri looked at him for a moment, pressing her lips together, and then turned around.

Yeonsu observed the two from a distance and chuckled to himself.

"A couple of lovebirds, I see," he murmured.

Danny and Yuri came back over, and the woman

greeted Yeonsu with an elegant gesture. As she turned to say goodbye to Danny, Yeonsu noticed a marking on the inside of her thigh, beneath her skirt. Some kind of pattern drawn in black ink.

Impressive.

Danny said goodbye to Yuri once more. Yeonsu had to drag him out. They boarded Danny's A-wing in the restaurant's parking sector. They set Yeonsu's apartment as the A-wing's destination, and started maneuvering in the air. The engine made a hissing sound.

As they flew toward the bridge, Yeonsu saw the white-haired man from the restaurant out in the street. He was clicking a small glowing device in his hand. The device continued to emit light sporadically.

What is that device? he thought, his brow furrowing. *Some kind of a signal?*

In the seat next to him, Danny had switched to autopilot and was leaning back to get some rest. Yeonsu considered waking him up, but decided to leave him be, and fell silently into thought himself. The white-haired man had already become a dot on the horizon, but Yeonsu couldn't take his eyes off that point. Perhaps it was his appearance, but a strange feeling tumbled in Yeonsu's stomach. What was this feeling?

A flickering light. Yeonsu had seen a similar device before. It was during his joint maneuver training as a lieutenant and a member of a combat squadron in Valhalla. All fighter jet formations always needed it before they could fly.

A photon beacon that dictated their destination.

It was something you would never see in Altra.

The next moment, Yeonsu shook Danny violently.

"Danny! Danny, wake up!"

Danny groaned and shifted his position. Yeonsu shook him even more violently.

"Wake up!"

"Ah… What is it? What's going on?"

Right as Danny opened his eyes, numerous dots appeared on the horizon, reflected on the A-wing's screen.

The dots grew bigger and bigger and transformed into the shape of airplanes. The aircrafts were moving up and down rapidly. Their cannons opened, revealing barrels of missiles.

The barrels began blowing fire toward the city.

Yeonsu and Danny watched the Jiangwei Bridge collapse through the back window. Shafts of the bridge facing the city fell to the ground in pieces. Citizens who appeared as dots to them could be seen running in all directions. Yeonsu's stomach flipped over and over as he stared in shock at the destruction.

Discarded had attacked Altra.

6.

"Danny, contact the troops!" Yeonsu shouted.

Yeonsu operated the communicator with the device on his wrist. He sent an emergency alert to his destroyer squadron stationed at a satellite base on New Shanghai's moon. Danny came to his senses and began sending communications to the Third Regiment. He sported an agility unlike someone who had just woken up. Yeonsu sent all kinds of emergency warning signals to headquarters and his squadron. *Please hurry.*

"Captain, over there!"

Yeonsu looked out the window at Danny's cry. He clenched his jaw.

"*Robespierre!*"

A large ship loomed on the horizon. A squadron of fighters were pouring out of the *Robespierre*'s dock.

Yeonsu's communicator rang with an alarm, and soon a voice spoke aloud, "Captain. This is Aiden."

"What's the situation?"

"As of now, 70 percent of the crew are on board waiting to depart from the moon."

"Kirox and Lu Xun?"

"They responded from Altra."

"Good. Aiden, you will act as the interim captain and lead the squadron to Altra. What about the other Command guards?"

"Currently, the Defense Forces outside the Shennong system are on the move. But it will take at least thirty minutes to an hour for them to reach Altra."

"Then we should be blocking the invaders. Damn it, when can we get there?"

"Our squadron will take about twenty minutes."

"Okay, see you soon," said Yeonsu. "Be careful, *Robespierre* appears to be fully armed."

"Understood, Captain. See you soon."

The comm line with Aiden ended.

"Captain, shouldn't we go to headquarters?" said Danny.

"Of course, Danny. How are we going to fight them now?"

Danny nodded and set the course to headquarters.

Then came a call from Harry Carlos. Yeonsu turned on the communicator again, and Harry's hologram appeared.

"Yeonsu, we've got a problem."

"Harry? Danny and I are seeing it now. We're heading to headquarters—"

"That's not urgent. Troops are being sent to the Alliance Research Institute."

A sense of dread swept over Yeonsu.

Harry spoke gravely. "Head there right away, Yeonsu. There's an *Admiral Cheng Ho* vessel there. Headquarters can't provide support because of the attack in the city. It's only held by the Third Regiment."

The flagship of the *Cheng Ho* Project, the *Admiral Cheng Ho* vessel. That was what the Resistance bastards were after.

Yeonsu fumbled to set the new destination coordinates.

"Captain, I'll go downtown," Danny cut in.

"What?"

"We need someone to protect the citizens. The people are defenseless. The police won't be able to stop them. I will join Lu Xun and Kirox here to protect the citizens."

A deep rage grew inside Yeonsu. He knew why Danny was acting like this and wanted to lash out at him, but he held back. Instead of shouting to his nephew that he was an idiot, he said in a very calm voice, "I know why you're doing this, Danny. But you don't have to. Yuri will be safe."

Danny's eyes widened. Yeonsu clicked his tongue.

"Yuri Ivanova is a part of the Discarded, Danny. You were deceived."

Danny's mouth fell open, but no words came out.

Yeonsu remembered the white-haired man and Yuri conversing. And the pattern tattooed on her thigh. He realized now what it was—a raven, the mark of the Discarded.

Why didn't I recognize that? he thought, grinding his teeth together.

"We're going to the research center," he said. "I'll explain as we go. Tell Kirox and Lu Xun to come to the lab too, Danny."

Kamura, *Robespierre's* land squadron instructor and captain, watched the fighter squadron ravaging the city with satisfaction. One of the fighters roared down in front of him. Kamura placed a photon beacon in his arms and watched it silently. The top cover opened and the Alpha Squadron leader, Mei Yang, appeared.

"Get in, Kamura," she said.

"Are you giving me a ride?"

Mei furrowed her eyebrows. "Think of it as an honor. I don't ride let just anyone ride on Emma."

"I'm so very honored."

Kamura burst out laughing and jumped into Mei's back seat. The fighter deck closed once again and took off.

The aircraft flew through low altitudes at a high speed. Mei fired plasma cannons, precision-guided bombs, and missiles at the city. Buildings collapsed and citizens screamed.

"How's the operation going?" she asked. "We can't go on forever like this."

"Of course," replied Kamura. "We're going to hit and run. Once their defenders show up, we'll be heading right back. This is their field, and a head-on collision would be suicide."

"Captain Joshua must be very happy."

"Does it need to be said?"

They both laughed.

A squadron of fighters crossed the city at high speed. In an instant, the city turned into a sea of fire. High-speed ships appeared from the other side of the Alpha Squadron—Altra's police ships. Mei gave orders to her squadron. Their fighter jets flew spread out at low altitudes, and the police ships seemed confused as they tried to maneuver between them.

That was their last flight. The scattered flying vehicles fired interceptor missiles at the police ships, which fell to the ground spitting fire.

Joshua nodded as he watched from *Robespierre*'s bridge.

"Now."

Cassie and the other concealed infiltrators who had been waiting above the research lab for the signal began to descend in a downward curve. Cassie's voice sounded through the comm link.

"I'll bring a gift for you soon, Joshua."

"Be careful, Cassie. If you must, retreat without hesitation.

"I have a good feeling about this," she answered. "You need to stop your worrying."

"Maybe."

Cassie let out a laugh.

The infiltration ships were huddled together and began spinning in a circle from the outer sides. As they continued to increase their speed, Gauss anti-aircraft guns appeared from all sides of the laboratory blowing fire. However, the anti-aircraft guns missed all the Discarded ships. It was an evasive maneuver unique to the Diutin-style fighter aircraft. Cassie was confident that the Alliance would not be able to capture their evasive maneuvers.

We acquired this skill with our blood, you bastards.

Cassie felt increasingly berserk as her adrenaline rose.

The anti-aircraft guns were all shattered by the missiles of the infiltrating ships. Chunks of scrap metal scattered through the air. The ships fired several plasma cannons toward the research facility.

The gap they'd created in the facility was getting bigger.

Lab personnel were screaming on the ground as they evacuated the building.

Soon after, the infiltrators landed in the courtyard.

Cassie debated shooting plasma cannons at the walls of the lab, but thought better of it. They didn't know where the ships equipped with wormhole generators were located.

Cassie disembarked with her crewmembers. Among them were Redhead Miyabe and the engineer, Kyungsu. The crew had been formed to take over the mysterious flagship equipped with the tech the Resistance and the Root Restorationists desired.

Miyabe stepped forward and scanned the lab with a mobile scanner system. After a moment, he pointed to a door at one corner of the building.

"This is the shortest route through the lab," he said. "Follow me."

Cassie nodded. Both she and her crew were wearing masks. They followed Miyabe through the doorway.

As they entered the lab and moved down the hallways, they saw numerous scientists, guards, and Allied soldiers running in panic. The place was in chaos, and it was easy for them to blend in and pretend they were also trying to escape.

"It's not here, but if we keep going this way, we'll enter another sector," said Miyabe after a few minutes. "I see a spot up there where it looks like they've gathered their ships. Let's go."

No one inside the building gave them any attention as they headed down a passageway at the center of the lab, toward the entrance to the next sector. Through open doors, Cassie spotted flasks and cluttered papers on tables.

In twenty minutes, she and her colleagues reached the end of the passageway. A man was struggling with a door that wouldn't open.

"Can you let us in?" she asked.

The man turned and looked at Cassie. Cassie smiled and lifted her gun.

"If you don't want to die."

The man raised his hands in fear.

"Who are you?" asked Cassie.

"Mahud Sakamoto, training officer."

"Okay, Mahud. If you're a training officer, you can open this door, right?"

Mahud blinked blankly and looked around at Cassie and her crew. His Adam's apple bobbed as he swallowed hard before nodding. "Yes, so don't kill me."

Miyabe laughed. "Open the door, Officer."

Mahud turned and walked over to the control system computer. Cassie and her crew kept their guns aimed at his back as he entered something into the machine. The control system let out a strange noise.

"The door won't open," said Mahud in a shaky voice. "I think something inside the system broke when you attacked us."

"Then hand over your lab control system source code. I'll take care of it."

Mahud's eyes widened. "That's—"

Miyabe silently placed his gun to the man's forehead. Mahud swallowed and nodded, looking humiliated.

"Okay. Open the source."

Miyabe activated the software of the multi-function electronic control unit mounted on his left wrist, and sent the software access path to Mahud. Mahud looked at him and typed the code into several computer screens. Cassie kept checking over her shoulder to make sure no one else would surprise them. It took a couple minutes for the new source code to download to Miyabe's control unit.

"It will be difficult with that alone," said Mahud.

"No, I can open the door with only this. Unlike you."

Miyabe struck Mahud's leg with his gun. The officer screamed and fell. Miyabe laughed.

"I won't kill you, as promised. But your luck will decide whether you die here or not."

He made several modifications to the lab source code. Soon he discovered a flaw in the system. The lab's inter-sector entrances were programmed to deactivate if even a single AA gun was destroyed. Miyabe corrected the code for that command and opened the door.

The heavy iron gate went up.

"Good job, Miyabe," said Cassie. "Shall we go in then?"

As soon as Cassie and her companions entered the next sector, they found guard droids advancing toward them.

"Spread out and hide!" Cassie cried.

Guard droids glided toward them and aimed their machine guns. Cassie hid behind the wall to the right of a nearby passageway. Her crewmembers did the same. But not all of them moved fast enough, and the droids targeted them with the machine guns. Bodies collapsed along with the *rat-a-tat* of the guns. The flash of blood and screams made Cassie flinch. She watched as the droids attacked the wall where the engineer Kyungsu was hiding, his eyes wide with terror.

"Miyabe! Hack those droids!" shouted Cassie.

But Miyabe couldn't raise his head at the constant pouring of bullets. Cassie clenched her teeth.

"How long does it take to hack them?"

"At least three minutes!"

Three minutes... Cassie felt her mouth go dry. She could also attempt to hack them, but she wasn't confident enough to do it faster than Miyabe. Cassie looked in the direction the other crew were hiding. There were two droids on their side, and one on Cassie's. The only person who could afford to act was Cassie.

She made up her mind.

Getting up from her position, Cassie fired an EMP at the middle of where the droids were standing. The bullets whizzed past her ear. It was a hair-raising sensation.

As the EMP field unfolded, it created dizzying electromagnetic field patterns. A droid near her collapsed with a mechanical sound. The other two droids shot the EMP fields with their guns as they fell, making the EMP bullets useless.

The droids focused their guns at Cassie. She swallowed.

"Hey, tin cans. Are you waiting for me?"

Cassie aimed her rifle at the droids and fired. The bullets bounced right off the droids.

They turned their upper bodies toward Cassie. It was time to run away. The droids' guns spewed fire, and Cassie leaped into the air. She jumped nimbly and landed on the ground in an acrobatic curve to avoid the gunfire, but her left arm became heavy. Blood was oozing from where the bullet had brushed her wrist.

Cassie groaned and started running. The droids followed her with sliding motions.

She dodged countless bullets as her breath began to shorten. In the next moment, Cassie realized she had reached a dead end. When she turned her head, she saw the droids had their guns pointed at her again. They were going to kill her and then kill the rest of the crew. Cassie couldn't escape them.

In the next moment, the two droids turned and fired

their barrels at each other. The droids were torn apart. But even in the midst of that, they did not stop their unfounded anger toward each other and continued to fire bullets at each other.

One collapsed and stopped functioning, and the other collapsed with a crackling sound. Cassie let out shaky laughter as she saw Miyabe and the others approaching from behind.

Miyabe sighed. "That was dangerous, Cassie." He held out his hand to help her up. "Can you move?"

"Sure. But I think we'll have to move a little faster, Miyabe."

Miyabe frowned in concern upon seeing her gun wound. At that moment, Kyungsu ran up to Cassie and stared intently behind her.

"Don't worry. I think we won't have to move much."

They all looked at Kyungsu, who pointed down a corridor Cassie hadn't noticed.

"Looks like the hangar is up ahead."

When Yeonsu and Danny arrived at the research center, they saw the destroyed anti-aircraft gun and the iron gate at the entrance. Danny soon met with Kirox and Lu Xun, who were waiting for them in the courtyard. Kirox handed Yeonsu and Danny each a set of protective gear and a phantom rifle. Kirox put on his goggles. Yeonsu put on his gear and, holding his rifle, spoke to the others.

"We're going in."

Yeonsu and the Third Regiment members quickly passed through Sector A. Danny was furious as he saw the mess inside the lab.

"I'm going to kill them."

They found a man lying at the entrance to sector B.

Danny recognized his trainer, Mahud.

"Officer!"

Mahud smiled sadly. "Isn't it a rough day today, Danny? It wasn't like this when you left this afternoon.

Danny saw the wound on his leg. "Don't speak. I'll call the medic."

The trainer shook his head. "A medic in this mess? Everyone's running away. If you delay any longer, you'll miss them. Go stop them, Danny. Lieutenant Colonel, do you understand what I'm saying?"

Yeonsu nodded, his face grave.

The officer's breathing turned harsh. "I'm sorry. I should have stopped them…but I ended up opening the door for them instead."

Mahud took one final breath before his head lolled to the side.

Yeonsu grasped Danny's shoulder. "Let's go, Danny."

He pulled Danny up from the ground.

"Let's go destroy them."

The radar on Mei's fighter jet detected a disturbing movement in the atmosphere. Altra's atmosphere was pulsing with a slight vibration as if it were minutes from a downpour. But it wasn't a raincloud. Through the clouds, giant metal figures began to appear. Movement on the radar turned into multiple dots. Alpha, Delta, Bravo, Charlie, and so on. It was the Star System Defense Force.

Mei observed the Allied ships filling the sky.

Kamura whispered from behind, "They're here."

Mei sent a message to *Robespierre*'s bridge: "The Star System Defense Force just showed up."

Joshua had also been watching. However, he had not yet

received any contact from Cassie's team. He weighed their situation.

"Leader of Alpha Squadron, they seem to be a sizeable fleet. It's trouble," said Joshua. He paused for a moment before continuing. "Can you buy me some more time?"

Mei was silent. The way her knuckles were turning white as she gripped the flight yoke, Kamura could tell she was nervous. It was the first time he had seen her like this.

"I will, Captain," Mei replied.

Joshua sighed. "I'm sorry, Leader. I'll send the Bravo Squadron for backup. Give me a little more time. I'll order a retreat soon."

Mei tried to remember where she had left her will. She had stopped writing it one day, as it had started to feel like an ominous superstition. Right at that moment, however, she regretted her decision. There had never been a moment when she was so desperate to write a will.

Alliance defense troops poured down from the sky. Five assault ships and cruisers took the vanguard. It was Yeonsu's Hound Dog squadron, led by Aiden. He planned to join the Star System Defense Force and exterminate the Discarded.

Several ships capable of spaceflight were lined up in the research center hangar. Cassie and the Discarded crew were amazed to learn that the hangar was larger than expected. About a dozen ships waited in the dock, most of them medium-sized and newer ships the size of a cruiser. Imagining these ships chasing after the *Robespierre* equipped with wormhole navigation left Cassie with great fear.

In the center of the dock was the largest ship. Its body was twice as large as that of other cruisers, and the clean special alloy material reflected all kinds of light.

Kyungsu stepped forward and read the inscription on the ship's body. "*Admiral Cheng Ho*? It looks like the name is *Admiral Cheng Ho*."

"*Admiral Cheng Ho*?" Miyabe frowned. "The first ship to lead an oceanic fleet to Earth?"

A memory came back to Cassie; she remembered reading that name in a history book about the motherland. Cassie knew that the *Admiral Cheng Ho* was the flagship of the Lightspeed Outer Space Exploration Project.

This was the ship that Karl Ryoma had been waiting impatiently to get his hands on. It was the result of the sacrifices of numerous refugees from the Mining Guild, including Cassie.

In her mind's eye, she saw the tombs of scrap metal and ships abandoned in the Dark Zone.

She had clung on to Yuna in the dark. Yuna, whose small body had trembled in her arms, crying, as she sensed her coming death. The ship had entered a gas storm and begun to crumble. Cassie's end had led her into a place of emptiness and death.

Lord, is this lonely and dark death really the end for me and my child? she had wondered.

The *Admiral Cheng Ho* was born from that thick cloud of death. Cassie listened to the ship come alive and speak to her.

Give me your blood and your flesh, and resurrect me.

"Cassie, we need to contact Captain Joshua."

Cassie blinked, coming to her senses. Miyabe was watching her, and the other crewmembers were preparing to enter the ship. She nodded and turned on her comm device. Still, with a fearful expression, she glanced at the ship's heavy body.

Joshua. We found the monster.

"Stop right there," said a voice behind her.

Yeonsu and members of the Third Regiment aimed their guns at the Resistance. The Discarded crewmembers also quickly raised their guns.

For a while, they stared at each other in that stance.

Yeonsu broke the silence.

"Don't be stupid. You guys are already finished. Automatic snipers already have you all within range."

Red laser points appeared on their foreheads.

Kirox, who was hiding behind the door leading to the laboratory at the top of the dock, grinned. His one-eyed goggle was facing one of the masked figures. Kirox was ready to pull the trigger at Yeonsu's command.

"Lower your guns without resistance. Make any move and all of you will die. White Raven, tell your men to put down the weapons."

Yeonsu smirked. "So, this is how the White Raven falls."

His voice was laced with the confidence of victory. Yeonsu also felt a sense of relief at the same time.

"Yeonsu?" said someone.

Yeonsu was startled, glancing around. No one among his crew would call out to him in this situation.

"Are you Yeonsu Jang?" said the voice again.

His eyes found the one who had spoken—the White Raven.

"Yeonsu Jang."

The Raven took off her white mask.

Yeonsu struggled to breathe.

"Cassie…Ice? Is that you, Cassie?"

7.

Cassie couldn't believe it.

He was looking at her, her first everything. The person she'd lost that day when hell unfolded, Yuna's father. The man who filled her youth. The name cried over and over in the wrecking ship as she clung to Yuna.

Yeonsu also couldn't believe what he was seeing.

He couldn't understand how his dead wife was looking at him with those eyes. What the hell kind of dream was this? His wife, Cassie Ice—a part of himself he'd lost during the Big Crush—was with the damned Discarded.

She was the White Raven.

Yeonsu felt like passing out. It felt like God was playing a bad joke.

Do you know how much I searched for you?

A strained voice came out of Yeonsu's mouth. "How are you…here?"

"And you…?" she said. "I thought you were dead."

Damn you, God. Are you laughing now? This had to be a

very comedic sight for him. Yeonsu didn't find this funny at all.

"Why?" he shouted.

Cassie shivered. Tears welled up in her eyes. "Why didn't you look for me?" she whispered. "I searched everywhere for you!"

"Cassie, I—"

Yeonsu wanted to shout all kinds of words, but he didn't know what would spill out. He wanted to say, *I looked for you for over twenty years. Every night when I go to sleep, I have nightmares of that day. No one knows how miserable my life has been without you. Ever since you disappeared, I've been a hollow shell.*

There had not been a single day in the twenty years since she'd disappeared from his life when he had not regretted that day.

It was a waking nightmare. Aircrafts pouring down from the sky; buildings collapsing; people dying. Eaters were hunting people. The smell of stale blood and burning flesh and sounds of gunfire; the sight of Cassie replaying over and over. He looked for her, but he couldn't find her anywhere, and the Eaters were approaching from behind.

Cassie. Cassie. Cassie. Cassie.

He was in a bungalow on a warm autumn afternoon. Was it their honeymoon? Cassie was looking down at him when he woke up. He saw Cassie's smiling face. Her smile always put him in a good mood. Without making a sound, she mouthed to him, "Let's have children." Yeonsu laughed. He hugged her and smelled her body. The scent of her body entered his nostrils and engrained itself in each of his olfactory cells.

Cassie. Cassie. Cassie. Cassie.

The woman who was more precious than his life was crying in front of him.

Men standing on both sides of the confrontation were equally as startled by the situation. Cassie and Yeonsu looked at each other without saying a word. Danny peered at the two of them in shock.

I cannot believe it.

The White Raven was the woman Uncle Yeonsu had told him about all those years ago. The only love of his life. Danny didn't know how to deal with this situation. Damn, who could have predicted this development?

At that moment, Danny realized that the White Raven looked much younger than Yeonsu. Confusion made his brow crease. As far as he knew, Yeonsu had been twenty-three years old at the time of the Big Crush, and his wife had been older than him. How could this happen?

Cassie's communication device rang loudly. It was Joshua.

"Cassie, I need you to hurry. The Star System Defense Force is here. Mei Yang and her squadron are fending them off, but they can't hold them back for much longer."

Cassie came to her senses and said, "I have to go."

"Where?" asked Yeonsu.

Cassie shook her head violently. "We have to go. We have to go, Yeonsu. Let us go."

Miyabe, who was standing behind Cassie, moved discretely.

A gunshot rang out.

Miyabe collapsed as he clasped his arms with a shriek.

"Stop shooting! Damn it, Kirox—don't shoot!" Yeonsu exclaimed.

Cassie glared at Yeonsu without looking back to Miyabe.

"You've become an Allied dog," she spat.

"Cassie, do you realize what you're doing? The Alliance saved us. They drove out the Eaters and rescued the Guild residents who had been ravaged."

Cassie laughed out loud. Yeonsu looked startled, but that didn't stop her. She smiled like a madman and wiped away her tears.

"Is that what those bastards say? That they saved the Mining Guild from destruction? That's funny."

Yeonsu didn't say anything.

"Captain Byungwook didn't tell you, Yeonsu? I know you spoke to him. It's the opposite. The Alliance was behind the attack on the Guild."

"Don't be absurd, Cassie. How could the Alliance move aliens at their will? They would never act on our orders." Yeonsu pressed his lips together. "Drop the gun, Cassie. I don't want to kill you."

"You think you can shoot me?" she snapped.

Yeonsu shut his mouth. He looked at her stubbornly. Cassie knew that expression.

Please, Yeonsu.

She was well aware that it would be difficult to stop Yeonsu when he made that face.

"I'll get you out somehow. But for now, drop the gun."

"I can't."

"You have to.

"Then I will die. The Alliance will kill me and my comrades."

"No, they won't. There's someone who can help, Cassie. I'll help you."

Cassie pressed her lips together and aimed her rifle at Yeonsu.

Yeonsu held a hand out. "Cassie, please."

"Yeonsu, did you know?" Cassie smiled twistedly. Tears streaked down her cheeks. "I don't care if I die here, because I've already died once ten years ago. If I die, I'd rather die at your hands anyway. So, choose. Shoot me or let us go."

Ten years? Yeonsu trembled as he thought carefully.

Danny pointed his gun from behind and whispered to Yeonsu, "Captain. Give me the order and I'll subdue them with my power."

"What?"

"It's the only way to capture them without losing any lives."

"You can apprehend that many people? What if you lose control?"

Danny didn't answer. He couldn't be certain.

In that fleeting moment, Yeonsu's mind ran a mile a minute.

What do I do? What do I do?

Could he shoot down everyone and save Cassie? Should he beg Harry to spare her?

Yeonsu made his decision and carefully spoke into the communicator to Kirox.

"Kirox, at my signal, kill everyone except the White Raven."

Cassie must've guessed what he was doing, because her eyes widened in horror.

"Yeonsu, no!" she screamed.

Yeonsu gave the signal. "Fire, Kirox!"

The bulkhead broke and a massive ship pushed into the dock hangar.

The hangar roared, shaking like crazy. Part of the wall poured down on the cruisers, damaging the bodies. Yeonsu and his troops lost ground and went flying from the shock.

When he landed, Yeonsu felt a warm substance dripping from his head. Blood. The crew entered his blurry vision. Lu Xun was nowhere to be seen, and Danny's flailed body appeared unconscious. Several people got off the ship.

A black man at the forefront of them shouted, "We'll take care of this. Get back to the *Robespierre!*"

Yeonsu could see Cassie and the Discarded moving about. Cassie turned her head and for a moment, she looked at him and said something.

What is she saying?

Before he could figure it out, Yeonsu lost consciousness.

"Karl brought backup. We are returning to *Robespierre* in the ship he came in."

Miyabe's communication sounded, and Joshua screamed with joy. Operations officers waiting on the bridge also embraced each other.

Joshua tried to speak calmly. "Good job, Miyabe. How long do you think you'll take to return?"

"I'd say about ten minutes."

"Okay."

Joshua nodded and gave orders through the operations officer.

"Alpha and Bravo Squadrons, return to the ship as fast as possible."

Mei gave orders to the fighter squadrons without delay.

"Alpha Squadron, head back to base! Bravo Squadron,

return as well."

"Roger that."

Squadrons flying around the city of Altra turned their noses.

Aiden shouted from *Little Boy*'s bridge, "Full speed maneuver! Shoot them all down!"

The Star System Defense Force, including *Little Boy*, opened their guns and fired at the fighters. About half of *Robespierre*'s fighter squadron was shot down.

Back aboard the *Robespierre*, the operations officer reported to Joshua.

"A group of high-speed boat units are moving from the command center to the research lab. Large cruisers were seen following at the rear of the high-speed boats. An infinity battleship was also reported."

"If there's a battleship, isn't it highly likely that it's the flagship of the Defense Command?"

"We haven't been able to determine its identity, but that seems possible, yes."

Joshua fell deep in thought, estimating the size of the squadron reported by the operations officer. It was too large for Karl Ryoma and his supporters to hold off. But Joshua couldn't go to help Karl when the *Robespierre* was also engaged with an enemy ship. Numerous Gauss railguns were firing at them. They were retaliating with plasma cannons, but the enemies were many and *Robespierre* was taking a lot of damage to the hull. The fighter squadrons and Cassie's separate squad had not yet appeared.

"We have an incoming communication from the enemy warship, Captain," said the operations officer.

"Put me through," Josha replied.

"Joshua Kwon. I'm Harry Carlos."

Joshua recognized the name. "The commander of the Allied Defense Force?"

"Yes. After all this time, this is how I've come to face you. You've underestimated the will of the Alliance government and your excellency, haven't you? You'll regret what you've done today. You're just a pack of abandoned wild dogs. I'll smash your teeth in so that you can't bark any more."

Joshua scoffed. "Oh, yeah? That's very scary. What are you going to do?"

"I'll present you with a sure death."

The radio cut off.

Joshua came to a decision. "As soon as the White Raven team and their aircraft returns, we are leaving the system."

The operations officer looked surprised, but nodded. "Understood."

Joshua noticed a small spherical merchant ship heading for the *Robespierre*. He exhaled a relieved breath. It had to be Cassie. He waited impatiently as her ship entered the dock.

Moments later, a squadron of fighters appeared. The Alliance cruisers had followed Cassie's ship.

Joshua gritted his teeth and exclaimed, "Recharge the plasma cannons! Fire at the enemy aircraft as soon as the rail guns are charged!"

Arsenal officers on the bridge rushed to ready the guns mounted on the *Robespierre*. Like any other day in New Shanghai, the sky was dyed a reddish hue from the evening sunset. Joshua cried out with sadness at the beautiful irony, "Fire artillery!"

Gauss rail cannon and plasma cannon fire ripped through the sunset, flying toward the Allied ships. The Allied fleet fired salvos right back at the *Robespierre*.

In the next moment, Joshua knew that something had gone wrong.

Cassie ran toward the bridge as soon as she disembarked. The ship was leaning to one side and the crew staggered behind her.

"Everyone to position!" Cassie yelled.

The crew all ran for their respective locations on her command. Miyabe headed to the communications room, and Kyungsu raced for the engine room.

When Cassie arrived at the bridge, she found Joshua staring wide-eyed at the flashing lights on the navigation screens.

"Joshua! The ship is shaking. What's going on?" she asked.

Before he could answer, a voice came over the ship comm link: "The starboard main engine and pathfinding module are on fire!"

Joshua let out a groan. "Damn it!"

The pathfinding module was *Robespierre*'s wormhole generator. If there was a problem with the wormhole generator, it would be impossible to escape the planetary system with a superluminal leap.

"Get us out of New Shanghai!" Joshua yelled to the chief engineer. "Full speed ahead."

The *Robespierre* began to move its heavy body toward the atmosphere, and the fighter squadrons followed. The Alliance assault ships chased after them like hyenas charging their prey.

Control personnel and crewmembers who lost balance due to the sudden movement let out a scream. Joshua looked to Cassie in distress. He felt that death was nearer than ever upon the evening sunset casting a romantic hue. In his mind, Joshua saw his wife, Jiyeon's, smiling face.

I never thought we would meet again so soon.

The atmosphere above New Shangai distorted with light. After a while, an oval-shaped ship appeared, ripping through Altra's sunset-filled sky. As if it had been there from the beginning.

Hypkeranos, Vice-Captain of the Adola System Defense Force, was experiencing déjà vu. This was the second time he had entered a human star system.

It was like this twenty years ago.

He saw the *Robespierre* on fire.

Your species is like a tiger moth, as you said, Joshua.

Hypkeranos radioed the *Robespierre*. In a moment, Joshua's hologram appeared.

Joshua spoke in disbelief, "Hyp?" He'd never been more shocked to see someone in his life. The Diutins had been the ones to supply and help transform the *Robespierre* ship. Their extraterrestrial race was known to the Alliance as the Eaters.

"My friend," said Hypkeranos. "Looks like you are in danger."

"Why have you come? Didn't the Diutinians decide to stop interfering with human affairs?"

Hypkeranos shook his head. "The council noticed that Diutinian technology was involved in a conflict in the human star system. They've summoned you to ours."

"What?"

"Do not resist, my friend. You must follow me."

Joshua looked visibly relieved that the Diutinians had come to save them. "Anything's better than dying here in vain," he said.

Hypkeranos's blue eyes gleamed.

Aiden stared with a gaping mouth at the newly appeared ship. He had never seen an Eater ship in person before, only on a video. Before long, the Eaters' ship emitted a blue light. Soon the light exploded, making Aiden shield his eyes with a hand. The unknown light looked like the same light that had appeared during the Big Crush. Is this…? *No, it can't be.*

Once the light went out, the *Robespierre*, a squadron of fighters, and several Allied ships had disappeared without a trace. In their place, the shades of the red sunset were the only thing left in the sky.

A deep fear pierced Aiden's bones. With a trembling hand, he signaled the ships to return home.

The Discarded's raid on Altra had come to an end.

8.

When Yeonsu woke up three days later, his head felt like it was going to crack open. He reached up and gently touched the bandage wrapped around it.

"You have a concussion," said the nurse at his bedside. "You need to be careful not to overdo it."

All Yeonsu cared about was learning what had happened to Cassie and the others. He soon found out that the White Raven was gone, but Commander Harry Carlos had captured Karl Ryoma and a group of Restorationists.

Yeonsu went to see Karl Ryoma as soon as he was able.

Karl was imprisoned in a straitjacket in a special Alliance camp created for major criminals. He smiled when he was led into the interrogation room where Yeonsu was waiting for him.

"Hello, Lieutenant Colonel Yeonsu Carlos. I'm Karl Ryoma."

Karl grinned. Yeonsu tilted his head, watching him.

"What's so funny?"

"It's funny that you're using the name Carlos. Isn't your real name Yeonsu Jang? I heard your conversation with the White Raven."

Yeonsu gave a blank expression. He observed Karl's appearance. It seemed he had already been interrogated at least once. Blood decorated his cheeks, along with traces of dried saliva. Harry was a diligent man when it came to his duties.

"I have something to ask you," said Yeonsu, clasping his hands behind his back.

"What is it?"

"Prophet Karl Ryoma. You preach humanity's return to Earth. Did you know about the *Admiral Cheng Ho* Ship before three days ago? You joined hands with members of the Discarded who knew of its existence."

"I did."

"How?"

Karl smiled bitterly. "That object belongs to the Mining Guild, Colonel Lieutenant. It's not the property of the Alliance. I've seen it before. During the Big Crush, twenty years ago."

It was difficult for Yeonsu to understand his words. Karl smiled as if he found Yeonsu's confusion funny.

"Are you from the Guild, Colonel? Do you know much about the Big Crush?"

"I experienced it directly."

"Looks like it. I listened in on you guys. The White Raven is your wife? Cassie Ice." Karl spoke seriously. "Did you know she has a daughter?"

Yeonsu felt as if he'd just been hit on the head. "What?"

Karl nodded. "Of course, you didn't. I thought so. Her daughter is about ten years old. I believe her name is Yuna.

But the child's father is not Joshua Kwon."

"You mean that child is my daughter?"

"I didn't say that, but Cassie believes so."

Only then did Yeonsu realize through his haze of memory what Cassie's last words to him had been.

You have a daughter.

Our daughter.

Yeonsu's body trembled.

"She's ten years old…? How can that be? If she were really my daughter, she would have to be at least twenty years old."

Karl looked at Yeonsu pitifully. He coughed and said, "Give me some water. I need to wet my lips."

Yeonsu considered his request and called for a glass of water. Karl put his mouth on the plate brought in by the guard and gulped it down.

After quenching his thirst, he spoke again. "Cassie Ice participated in the Alliance's outer space exploration project several times. She had to in order to survive on the devastated planet. There was a project that analyzed the engines of captured ships to test the performance of various randomly created engines. Do you know of that project?"

The pieces came together in Yeonsu's mind. By participating in the project, Cassie and his daughter had been affected by Einstein's time paradox. *The closer you get to the speed of light, the more relative time gets for observer and subject both.*

While ten years had passed for Cassie, out in the far reaches of space, twenty years had passed for Yeonsu.

Cassie, you never showed your face. No matter how much I searched, I could not find you. I didn't get to see you grow old. I didn't even know my daughter was born. Now, after twenty years, you're both White Raven and Cassie Ice, and my daughter is ten years old? This is what I have to accept now?

Yeonsu felt a laugh rising out of him. But this wasn't funny at all.

At the time of the Big Crush, his age was twenty-two and Cassie was twenty-five. Now he was forty-three, and Cassie was probably around thirty-five.

Karl looked at Yeonsu's bewildered expression. "Lieutenant Colonel?"

Yeonsu put his face in his hands and sobbed. Tears flowed endlessly down his cheeks.

Karl watched Yeonsu cry without saying a word.

After a while, he spoke calmly. "Now, I will tell you the truth, Colonel. The Big Crush was the result of the first three ships equipped with wormhole technology developed by the Mining Guild, the *Incheon*, the *Gunsan*, and the *Los Angeles*. They entered the star system of the Diutin people on their first mission. The Diutin government misunderstood the arrival of the three ships as an invasion, and began an attack. In an instant, the *Gunsan* and *Los Angeles* ships were shot down, and the *Incheon* ship created a wormhole back to planet Han and escaped. As you have seen, the moment you make a wormhole, a bright light is emitted like you've never seen before."

A memory flashed in Yeonsu's mind—the supernova explosion before the Eaters appeared.

A blue light generated by the wormhole generator.

"Diutin's army chased *Incheon* and rode that wormhole to Han. To prevent a potential threat, and also because they were scared. They never thought they would meet an alien race with warp-drive technology, I guess."

Karl's face gradually turned pale and his breathing became rough. Yeonsu looked up and saw the traces of tears on his face, just like his own.

"I am Karl Age. At the time, I was an interpreter dispatched by the Alliance to the Mining Guild's outer space alien exchange project at the order of Lieutenant Colonel Harry Carlos. I was assigned to the *Incheon*. And at his order, I sent a manipulated transmission to the Diutin ship."

What? Yeonsu felt a sudden anger as he looked at Karl.

"Harry? Transmission? What transmission were you sending?"

Karl spoke painfully, "'We are mankind of the Desirée system, and we have come to subdue you. If you do not express surrender, we will burn down the Diutin motherland.'"

Yeonsu shot up so quickly that Karl couldn't defend himself. He grabbed Karl Ryoma by his collar and threw him to the ground. The table broke with a loud *bang*. Karl groaned, unable to breathe as Yeonsu wrapped his hands around his neck.

Yeonsu glared at his chin with murderous eyes. "You bastard, quit your bullshit."

Saliva dripped from Karl's chin, and he couldn't speak a word. Yeonsu, who had been strangling his neck without hesitation, relaxed his hands. Karl inhaled deeply several times. Yeonsu watched without saying a word. He was trembling with anger.

Karl Ryoma swept his restrained hands around his neck and glanced at Yeonsu.

Yeonsu was silent as he looked down at the floor. Then he spoke in a hoarse voice.

"My father, Harry Carlos, gave you the orders?"

Karl coughed. "That's right, Colonel."

"Can you prove it?"

At that, Karl started laughing. His laugh rang through the entire interrogation room. It was a terrifying sight. A terrorist in a straitjacket smiling madly, and an Allied lieutenant colonel sitting with a somber expression. Yeonsu wanted to tear Karl Ryoma apart. But at the same time, he wanted to cling to his legs and cry. He continued to listen to Karl's laughter.

His laughter had faded, but he was still giggling.

"What's so funny?"

"You don't find it funny, Colonel? You, who should hate Harry Carlos more than anyone, call him father."

Karl's voice turned dark in an instant. His mood continued to fluctuate as his gaze met Yeonsu.

"There hasn't been a single day that I didn't regret it, Colonel. What I've done. That's why I'm trying to bring down the Alliance and preach for our return back to Earth. I regret it! And I despise him—your father, Harry Carlos. That murderer!"

Veins bulged in Karl's eyes. He smiled again, but his eyes remained red.

"Doesn't it feel futile? He saw me, but he didn't remember me. Has it been that long? I remember it all so well. I can't ever forget that day!"

Yeonsu felt deeply tired. He rubbed his eyes. "Again, can you prove it, Karl? What you just said."

Karl stopped laughing madly and looked at Yeonsu with swollen eyes, blazing with anger.

"Look through Harry's personal computer. You'll find the Karl Age records deleted from the Allied database. Search by my codename at the time."

"Codename?"

Karl replied, "Emissary of the Stars."

9.

Harry Carlos was on his way back to his office after a Command general meeting. There was a pounding in his head. The commanders of the first, second, and third regiments of the Star System Defense Forces and the Joint Chiefs of Staff had continued to argue about the existence of the Eaters. They had finally reached a consensus: the Eaters were a threat to humanity, and a freshly developed wormhole generator should be installed on all ships.

Harry clenched his teeth. *Those idiots.*

That technology had just now been "recovered." They would need more time to be able to mass-produce it. Why had the Eaters appeared? That's what he still couldn't understand.

Were the Diutinians working with the *Robespierre*?

Harry entered the office. He found his desk and turned on the light.

With a sigh of exhaustion, he unbuttoned his uniform and took some wine out of the small refrigerator before returning to his desk.

As he poured the wine into a glass, he sensed something was different about the desk.

Harry turned on his monitor. Someone had tampered with his computer. The system was waking up from sleep mode. He looked at his surroundings while opening the desk drawer.

His gun was missing.

"You look very tired, Harry."

The silhouette sitting on the bed in the dark turned into Yeonsu Carlos. Harry felt like he was watching magic. The silhouette raised its upper body.

"Yeonsu. You surprised me."

"I'm sorry. I guess you're back from a meeting. Did you find the Discarded?"

"Don't get me started. The Discarded aren't the problem. Command is in a state of panic because of the Eaters appearing again after twenty years. Those ignorant old men. They talk about things they've never even seen. Some say we have to attack with a low warp drive. Can you believe it?"

"I guess they're scared. People are afraid of what they don't know."

Harry Carlos thought of the Second Name War. A storm that had engulfed his youth. People who died and killed each other because of their names.

"That's right, son. Cowards."

"Is there anything about you that I don't know, Harry?"

Yeonsu got up from the bed. Harry spotted his missing gun in Yeonsu's hand.

"Yeonsu."

Yeonsu aimed the gun at Harry. Looking into Yeonsu's

eyes, Harry realized this wasn't a joke.

Yeonsu was prepared to shoot him.

Harry swallowed hard. "What did you see?"

"Your real face."

"What do you mean?"

"Emissary of the Stars, remember?"

"What? Who told you that phrase?"

"Do you remember Karl Age, Harry?"

Harry shut his mouth. Yeonsu laughed at his expression.

"You seem to remember. I searched the computer a bit. But you don't seem to remember his face."

Harry frowned. "It was twenty years ago. Can you really expect me to remember everything that happened so long ago?"

"Karl Ryoma. Look at his face again." Yeonsu chuckled darkly. "If there is a chance—"

Yeonsu stopped talking, shaking his head in disgust. Harry's heart beat fast as he measured the distance from his chair to the door, but he couldn't see how he would get out in time. Yeonsu could kill him in an instant.

"So, that was Karl Age. It may have been a big discovery for you, but it's very boring to me."

Yeonsu spat, "Why did you do it, Harry? Why did you let so many people die?"

Harry looked at him silently. Yeonsu felt an unbearable thirst. He wanted to pull the trigger. *Can't I just pull it?* But he couldn't.

"Are you going to shoot me, son?"

"I am not your son."

Harry, the bold Harry. During the Big Crush, Harry had organized a detached unit to rescue refugees from the Mining Guild. He had been the youngest man to be promoted to military rank. Harry, the commander of the second regiment in the Alliance Command's Star System Defense Force, and commander of the Outer Space Exploration Project.

And Harry the murderer who'd allowed tens of millions of people to be blown to smithereens.

"Did you also select personnel for the Lightspeed Outer Space Exploration Project?"

Harry looked into Yeonsu's eyes and the muzzle of the gun.

He'd gone looking for volunteers himself, traveling across the planet Han in search of victims.

"You took Cassie Ice from me, my wife." Yeonsu snarled.

"The kid wanted it."

Yeonsu's eyes widened.

"Are you surprised? To be honest, I remember them all. The victims. Karl Age? The guy altered his face. It wasn't like that before. Outer Space Exploration Project? I remember every single volunteer. They were weary bastards tired of living. I gave them a dream. I gave a future to those who couldn't even see past their tomorrow. The child wanted it. Their livelihood was urgent."

"Can you say that to the people of the Mining Guild? You, who destroyed their tomorrow? 'I took your future away, but I can give you a future again! I am the Star God, Guardian of the Desirée, the all-powerful Harry Carlos!' Isn't that so much fun, Harry?" Yeonsu's eyes were wild as he shouted and gestured with his unarmed hand.

Harry frowned. "Stop this."

"No! Twenty years have passed and I just discovered this comedic play. We should enjoy it more! How can you not? Harry, can you do that?"

In his mind, Yeonsu pictured a burning horizon. Ships that appeared in the sky poured down like rain, slaughtering people.

A young Cassie yelling at him for help.

Yeonsu saw a sticky darkness of unknown depth obscuring his vision.

"*Admiral Cheng Ho*? I guess that's the *Incheon*. Oh my God, it was that one ship with a damn wormhole generator that killed tens of thousands of people?"

This was the truth. That in order to secure superluminal outer space navigation technology, the Mining Guild had been destroyed and the *Incheon* ship had been stolen.

Harry's detachment was not sent to Han to save people, but to take advantage of the *Incheon*.

Now, the *Incheon* was preparing to depart after completing repairs at the dock of the Alliance Research Institute.

Admiral Cheng Ho.

Yeonsu pointed at himself with the gun. "Why did you adopt me? For what? Why did you make me this way?"

He remembered Harry when he was young. A righteous Harry, who was more heartbroken than anyone at the deaths of civilians. What was all of that but a lie?

"Because Sean tried to save you."

Yeonsu thought of dead Sean. Danny's father. An infinite sadness flooded him.

"I saw myself in you," said Harry. "A young man who had lost everything, collecting the corpses of his parents who died because of a name. So, I saved you."

"Really? Why don't you try to save yourself again, Commander Harry Carlos?"

Yeonsu aimed at Harry.

Bang!

A gunshot rang out. Smoke rose from the gun barrel. Harry ignored the blood dripping from his left cheek.

The bullet had missed.

"You can't shoot me."

Yeonsu looked down at his hand holding the gun. He pointed again at Harry and fired.

It missed again; the bullet only punctured the wall behind Harry.

Harry stared at him, expressionless.

"Ahhhhhhhh!" Yeonsu screamed. He kicked the desk. Harry's computer and console shattered with a *crunch*. Yeonsu kept smashing the objects in the room. He hit papers with his hands, used the desk legs to smash glass, and snapped the portrait on the desk in half and kicked at it. And still he continued to shout and bellow, as Harry watched silently.

A maddening silence followed.

After a painful moment, Yeonsu opened his mouth. His tone was strangely calm and sad.

"Does Danny know?"

Harry shook his head. "No."

"That's good. For me, for Danny, and for you, Harry."

Yeonsu clenched his teeth as something inside him trembled. "Don't ever tell that child. Ever."

"I wasn't planning on it. There's no need to trigger his unstable mind."

Yeonsu opened the gun magazine, spilled the contents, and kicked them under the bed. He trudged to the door and opened it.

"What are you planning to do?" asked Harry.

"It's none of your business."

Harry called out toward Yeonsu's turned shoulder,

"Yeonsu."

Yeonsu turned around. He looked at Harry with tears in his bloodshot eyes. "If you call my name one more time, then I will really kill you."

Harry didn't say anything. He knew instinctively that Yeonsu was not coming back.

"Where are you going?"

"Far. Very far. Somewhere I can get away from this disgusting gutter," Yeonsu mumbled back. He slammed the door shut behind him.

IO.

Karl lay in the dark with his body hanging haphazardly in his straitjacket. His mouth was dry and his limbs and back were screaming, but he didn't care.

Can you interpret for the aliens, Karl? It's a very simple job, said Harry Carlos, who appeared from the darkness.

Karl saw the ambition in that man's eyes. A dangerous ambition that had corroded Karl's mind for the rest of his life.

Karl remembered people burning. Burning and melting from the inexplicable violence inflicted by the aliens that appeared in the sky.

Man, woman, elderly, child, dog, cat, and tree.

All were burning.

I didn't want this.

Karl saw a gigantic star. A star that emitted darkness, not light. He felt the suffocating pain, and unseen darkness set his body on fire.

The darkness engulfed him.

He wanted death. The purest kind of death that could bring him salvation.

A strange sound reached his ears. Urgent footsteps and gunshots. The sound of footsteps appeared to move away, but soon came closer. Karl listened quietly.

Smoke entered his room. Something unusual was happening.

Yeonsu Carlos kicked open the door to the cell and shouted, "Karl, come out!" He was wearing a gas mask.

All kinds of people were heard moving outside the door.

"What the hell is this, Colonel?" asked Karl.

"I'm doing what you were meant to do. Terrorism is a very refreshing feeling. A good way to relieve some stress. If I'd known it was like this, I would've done it sooner."

Karl didn't understand any of Yeonsu's words. "What was I going to do?"

"Meet the *Admiral Cheng Ho.*"

Karl opened his mouth. Yeonsu held out the gas mask to him.

"Go to Earth, Karl. With your people." Yeonsu laughed when Karl just stared at him. "Are you going or not? I thought I'd take a trip to cool off as well."

Yeonsu swiftly freed the rest of Karl's supporters. He left the guards lying on the floor with gunshot wounds. He then led Karl and his supporters to the back of the camp toward the hangar. At an intersection near the middle of the path, Yeonsu turned to Karl.

"Go and embark, Karl. Here's the *Admiral Cheng Ho*'s embarkation command protocol." Yeonsu held out a multi-function control device in the form of a glove, which Karl placed on his left wrist. "I'm going to take care of the rest of the guys who followed us, so go and get the ship ready. I'll meet you soon."

When Yeonsu turned around, Karl said, "Wait."

Yeonsu looked back at him.

"Don't die, Colonel Carlos."

"I'm no longer Carlos, Karl. Call me Yeonsu Jang."

"Okay, Lieutenant Colonel. I'll be preparing her for maneuver, so come soon."

Yeonsu nodded and hurried off.

Arriving in the hangar, Karl found the *Admiral Cheng Ho*. The vessel stood still, unaffected by the commotion. Karl boarded the ship with his companions. It didn't take them long to finish preparations for departure. They waited quietly for Yeonsu.

Even if he returned, would he become Karl's ally? Karl wasn't sure. The man had been thrown naked into the pit of truth, and Karl had no idea what that would lead a man to do.

A man with a rifle appeared in the hangar. It was Yeonsu.

Karl Ryoma smiled. Yeonsu approached the *Admiral Cheng Ho* and shouted, "Passenger Yeonsu Jang, requesting to board."

"Where is your destination?"

"Earth."

"Welcome, Yeonsu Jang."

After he was on board, the ship dock closed. A blue light was emitted into the air near the engine bay.

The light gradually grew larger into the shape of a sphere, distorting the space around it. A force field unfolded around the *Admiral Cheng Ho*. The force field gradually coalesced and turned into a cylindrical shape.

It was a deep, blue passage that no one could see through. A soft blue light spread in all directions.

The engine of the *Admiral Cheng Ho* spewed fire. Soon the ship disappeared into the passage.

Darkness fell again.

When Cassie returned to her room, Yuna was reading a history book. She closed the book upon seeing her mother. Cassie sat down and started braiding Yuna's hair. The mother and daughter did not speak for a while. For Cassie, the time she had to braid her child's hair was precious and comfortable.

"Did you see my biological father?" asked Yuna.

Cassie's stomach dipped. "Where did you hear that?"

"Uncle Joshua told me. He said you were very sad and tired, so he told me to take care of you."

Yuna turned her body to look at Cassie. As she looked into her daughter's clear eyes, sadness spread through her body. Here was a child who'd grown up without a father. The child understood her mother's sorrow from an early age and knew how to accept it quietly. In the Dark Zone, Yuna had patted Cassie on the back even while trembling in fear.

Since when had this child become so mature?

Cassie felt tears welling up in her eyes, but she smiled. "Yuna, you've grown so much. Even more mature than me. Yeah, I met your dad. We both thought the other was dead. One for ten years, and the other for twenty."

"Because of time distortion?"

"That's right. Sometimes the universe picks at those who are weak, Yuna. Your father may have longed for us more than we did for him. He grieved for a much longer time." Cassie recalled Yeonsu's eyes looking at her like a wounded animal.

Yuna hugged Cassie and buried her face in her chest. "What's my dad's name?" she asked tearfully.

Cassie patted the girl on the back and whispered into the ear of her treasure, "Yeonsu Jang. That's how we placed our surname in our homeland."

Then our Yuna will become Jang Yuna, or Yuna Jang, Cassie thought to Yeonsu.

Yeonsu stood on the bridge as he saw a group of lights moving to and fro, blinding his eyes. He did not remember the light from twenty years ago being so bright. He saw Cassie's face through the light, and Danny's as well. He saw the planet Han, full of ruins.

He saw Cassie in the bungalow, smiling as she murmured, *Let's have children.*

He hugged her tightly. Ten years for her, and twenty years for him passed through the light in an instant. Yeonsu knew then that he was navigating against time.

When he reached the end of the light, Yeonsu stood at a place where all sound had disappeared, alone.

It lasted only a moment, and then all kinds of nebulae unfolded before his eyes. A shining star appeared in the distance. It was the sun, the burning star that gave birth to the original human race.

Yeonsu saw a nebula. Somewhere in there was the Desirée system, and other unknown star systems as well. The *Robespierre* and Cassie would certainly be there.

Yeonsu hoped his voice could reach the nebula, to cross through the eons of time and space and finally reach her.

Finally, for the last time.

I love you, Cassie.

Tears poured out of his eyes.

The nebula shone tens of thousands of lights fractured on Yeonsu's cheeks.

Part 2

Resistance

I.

A fishy smell filled the air. The endless ocean spewed bub-
bles to and fro. Tentacles appeared and disappeared among
the whirlpools of seawater. Even at noon, the old sun, scat-
tering its red light, was watching this scene.

A dome sat in the middle of the sea. Inside the dome,
marble structures stood facing the sky, watching the waves
crashing above the dome.

Drops of blood slowly dripped down from the marble.

Two men with their side hair shaved appeared with
a woman, on the path outside the dome. The woman
was supporting one of the men, and the man behind
them advanced while holding a rifle and checking their
surroundings. A moan escaped through his mouth. He felt
faint, but he didn't stop moving.

If they stopped, he would never run again.

A circular assault ship lowered alongside their path.

The woman cried, "The corpses are gone!"

The vigilant man at the back said, "We need to get out

of here quickly, Yukyung. Prepare for takeoff immediately! Be sure to quarantine that friend."

The staggering man leaning on the woman's shoulder let out a moan. The woman said, "What about you?"

"I'll have your back while you board the ship. Go!"

The woman pulled the man to her by his collar and kissed him. "Yeonwoo, don't die, okay?"

The man nodded, and the woman, still supporting the man, struggled to approach the ship.

After the woman and the injured man disappeared, Yeonwoo raised his rifle and looked around again. Sweat dripped down his face. Huge blue waves hit against the outside of the dome, making a sound.

Splash!

Through the sound of the waves, he heard strange noises. The sound of something dragging and moving on the ground.

Corpses missing their lower body were approaching him.

Those corpses had been his companions until a few hours ago.

Counting to three, Yeonwoo loaded plasma ammunition and raised the plasma temperature of the rifle. Plasma flew toward the corpses, splattering them into pieces.

Meanwhile, Yukyung placed the injured man down near the back of the ship's cockpit. Taking hold of the control stick, Yukyung turned on the engine. It vibrated as it came to life. More than half of the fuel tank was left. She prepared for a sub-light flight mode.

She called to Yeonwoo, who stood outside the ship with his back to the speaker. "Come back now!"

Yeonwoo nodded. He carried his rifle behind him and

ran. No, he *tried* to run.

The battered corpses combined together to form a large body.

It approached Yeonwoo.

Yukyung screamed. "No!"

The corpse mass elongated. Yeonwoo aimed his rifle and fired at it. Human limbs sprayed in pieces, spewing blood.

"Go, Yukyung! Let's go!"

Yukyung opened the cannon door of the ship. Through the scope that appeared in the window, she aimed at the monster and pressed the button frantically. Cannons rotated and fired high-temperature plasma into the monster, disassembling it. Yeonwoo was covered in blood. He wiped at his eyes and headed for the ship.

Yeonwoo felt a terrible pain in his belly.

Something was sticking out from his upper stomach. A transparent blade that moved like it was flowing. When he turned his head, he saw a red-eyed alien. The alien took back the sword that appeared from the device on his left wrist, and Yeonwoo fell, bleeding from his mouth.

"No…" murmured Yukyung as the corpse came together again. The corpse monster loomed in front of Yeonwoo's collapsed body.

The monster lifted Yeonwoo's shaking body, opened its long snout, and slipped Yeonwoo's body inside its mouth.

It chewed.

Yukyung looked at the scene blankly.

Soon after its meal, the monster fixed its eyes on the ship. The alien also peered at the spaceship. Shadows of more corpses emerged from behind them. Hundreds of corpses.

With trembling hands, she activated the sub-light flight.

The spaceship began to emit a light as it soared vertically toward the sky.

All sorts of small asteroids and space debris surrounded the spaceship as it fled the atmosphere. The spacecraft had left the sea planet and was leaving the system at 20 percent of the speed of light.

Yukyung fell into despair, drooping her body in the cockpit. Yeonwoo was dead. She wanted to scream and weep.

A rattling sound came from behind.

Yukyung flinched and lifted her head. Sweat had dripped down her face. *Pull yourself together.*

The man she'd brought in was not quarantined. She looked to the back of the cockpit where'd she left him.

He had disappeared.

Yukyung quietly picked up her automatic pistol.

It wasn't over yet.

"Look at that fire. It is a savage fire that has burned civilization and swallowed it up in its dark stomach. We must have cut off one of the buds of the noble civilization that Mother Universe has nurtured today.

How can that sin be washed away?

Until the day we change, we will be forever cursed…"

—Excerpt from the logbook of Hypkeranos,
Vice-Captain of the Adola Defense Force,
right after the air strike on a planet

2.

Her father took her and her sister once a year to a villa in Anji Valley, three hours from the capital. Every year since she was two years old, when she started to speak the word "dad." Going to the villa was a precious ritual. The year was divided into before and after going there. At the villa, she saw the stars, slept near the fire, and heard many stories that cheered up the stillness of the night. When it was past midnight, her father told her stories about the suns and constellations of other worlds that shone from afar, while she ate the spicy noodles and bbq he'd made.

Sleeping in her hammock, she had many dreams. In her dreams, she saw ships cutting through the universe. The ships were running through empty space and time, radiating a lonely light through the eons of darkness. She saw the pioneers in the story and the legendary extraterrestrial life that was now gone.

One day, she dreamed of a creature swimming in the vast darkness. The all-white giant creature looked like a primordial sea creature from a sea planet in an old frontier story she had heard from her father. It had a long neck, a blunt-looking body, and six legs. But the creature had a mysterious beauty. Above all, its eyes were beautiful. Surrounded by multiple layers of haze, its eyes were filled with all kinds of brilliance. She was mesmerized, looking into those eyes. The creature swam without even looking at her.

Then the darkness tightened around the creature. Slowly but surely. She was about to scream. She couldn't do a thing as the darkness expanded its realm, finally engulfing the struggling creature's body. The light of life dimmed in its beautiful eyes. It looked very frightening.

When she woke up, she found herself crying. Tears flowed uncontrollably, and her shoulders shook. Her father came over and held her in his arms.

"Shh, Yurina. What's going on? Why are you so upset?"

She told her father about the creature in her dream. About the beautiful marine life encroached in the darkness, and its eyes. About the darkness that tried to turn off the light.

"Yurina, it was only a dream. The darkness in a dream can never do anything to you."

He patted daughter's head and continued to rub her shoulder.

"Remember, daughter, your sister and I are always by your side, so the darkness can't do anything to you."

She nodded and went back to sleep without realizing it. Hoping to see marine life again. She'd forgotten the darkness in the dream already.

There was such a day.

And her father disappeared into darkness.

A dry wind blew over the Balthazar Plateau.

Grasses sprung up and swayed between the red soil.

The wind remembered everything. Everything since the creation of this plateau. The footsteps of men and women worried about the future. The sigh and love of the young shepherds. War, death, and blood. Sometimes history would interfere in that way, but mostly, time stood still on the plateau.

All that time, the wind was there.

The wind saw a dust cloud at one end of the plateau.

The enlarged object turned into the outline of a hover bike with a sleek carbon body. A long cloud of dust rose from the bottom of the bike.

The wind was curious about who was coming. The occupant of the hover bike was a slender woman with short hair. She wore windproof binoculars and a mask.

The woman raced at the highest speed over the rocks dotting on the plateau, without even slowing down.

Three men watched her from afar.

The bike slowed down. The engine noise quieted, and the woman jumped off. One of the men, who appeared to be the oldest, took a step closer. He had an impressive cut on his left eye. A holster hung from his waist. The men in the back had their rifles hanging down.

"It's been a while, Yuri."

The woman took off her mask. "It's been a while, Jena. Is your wife healthy?"

"She's fine," the man replied stiffly. "I'd rather hear about what you've been up to."

"Sometimes life can be fun or it can be annoying. It's entirely up to you to decide."

"Are you here to say hello or make an offer?"

"Both. How is Karan?"

"Eating well, working hard. I'm very sorry that I haven't contacted you for a long time. Are you ready to meet him?"

"I always thought this moment would come, Jena."

Jena looked at Yuri for a moment with an unknown eye and then nodded. "Okay."

At the end of the plateau, a shabby one-story brick house appeared. The wind was startled. It had seen this house before, but it was always strange to see the house disappear and reappear.

"Wow, it's well hidden," said Yuri.

"Come in, Yuri. If we take too long, they'll catch you. It looks like nobody is there, but we don't know who's watching us."

The wind's heart was pounding. Yuri took a deep breath and grabbed the doorknob of the house.

The woman vanished.

The wind was mesmerized. The men jumped on their hover bikes and manipulated them a few times. Soon the other bike entered the warehouse on the side of the brick house on its own. Jena nodded at the men with rifles. They disappeared, and Jena was left alone. The wind thought, *What the hell are they doing?*

Jena suddenly stared at a place on the plateau. He was staring at the wind.

He muttered something, turned, and grabbed the door-knob.

Jena disappeared, and so did the brick house.

The wind wondered when it would see them again.

When Yuri entered the house, she was faced with an internal structure that was completely different from what she had seen from the outside. The house was on the fifth floor, and as she walked through a clean hallway, an elevator appeared.

A man in a white suit, with neatly combed hair, was standing in front of the elevator.

"Hello, Yuri. The boss is waiting for you."

"Where am I going, Judy?"

"Top floor," said the man. "Just go in and press the button for the fourth floor."

"Isn't it the fifth floor?"

"If you press the fifth floor, you will go back to the place you were before."

"Okay."

The elevator arrived. The door opened, revealing a silver interior. Yuri got on and pressed the button for the fourth floor, and the door closed.

When the elevator door opened again, Yuri saw a table set with full-course meal.

"Yuri Ivanova," said the man sitting before it.

"Karan Shetty."

Karan Shetty smiled and pointed to the seat opposite him. "You haven't eaten? Sit down."

"I'm not really hungry."

"Sit," he said again. "You're here because you need me? I like to chat while eating. You know?"

Yuri thought for a moment, then took off her goggles and sat across from Karan Shetty.

"Trust me, Yuri. It'll be delicious." Karan took a fork and knife and started slicing the meat.

The plate before Yuri held salad with roast potatoes, salmon steak, and cheese. Her stomach growled at the smell. Karan smiled as she started to finger her fork.

"When did you come to Valhalla?" he asked.

"It's been a few days."

"Has it been three years?"

"Four years."

"I didn't expect you to be in touch as soon as you arrived, but it's all right. I've always wondered how you're living. Don't you miss us? I thought you'd miss us."

"I miss you, Karan. How can I forget you?"

"Liar."

Yuri stopped the fork. "Karan."

"You never missed us, Ivanova. Did you think I didn't care that you left us to join the Resistance and do all sorts of outrageous things? You abandoned your family."

"I have no family, Shetty."

"We were your family, Yuri."

Yuri captured Karan Shetty's calm and intelligent facial features. He had always been a quiet man. However, there was no one in Valhalla who did not know there was heat hidden within his silence.

"Eat, Yuri. Let's talk while eating."

Yuri put down the fork. "Karan, I have something to tell you."

"Let's eat and talk. I haven't finished eating yet."

"Help me, Karan. I need your help."

"Yuri."

"There will be a revolution."

Karan Shetty's black eyes stared at her.

"When that day comes, we need the help of our brothers, Karan."

Karan Shetty finished the meal. Judy and Jena came in. The

empty table was filled with Karan Shetty's henchmen in an instant. Some of them looked surprised at the sight of Yuri, but most didn't look at her at all.

Karan Shetty lit a cigarette. "Brothers, our comrade Yuri Ivanova is back."

All the men who had deliberately turned away from her looked at her. Warriors. They were brothers who'd crossed the line and shared death on the red wind.

They were men of wind raised by the barren planet Valhalla.

"He who has abandoned his brother cannot become the red wind again," said the man with a tangled face, Theresia. He was the most stubborn of Karan Shetty's men.

"She didn't forsake us, Theresia," Gain said. He was relatively young, and he had been taught how to shoot by Theresia as a child. Yuri expressed her thanks with her eyes. "She has only left us for a while for the sake of her beliefs. You know? She's fighting the Alliance government on our behalf. What did the Red Wind do while Yuri Ivanova was doing that?"

"You'd better be careful with your words, Gain. Don't insult your brothers!"

"Would you like me to pull out that good tongue?"

Some of the men stepped forward with threatening looks in their eyes, clenching their fists. Karan Shetty didn't even look at them, as if he wasn't interested in them.

Theresia looked at Karan. "Captain, are you going to accept her as the daughter of the wind again?"

The men raised their voices at each other, some insisted that they accept her again, and others saying they could not accept her.

Karan covered his ears at the noise and shrugged. "

Well, Theresia, don't you think she wants that? Let's listen to Yuri. Everyone be quiet, quiet!"

Jena smashed the wooden table. The men gradually shut their mouths.

"Everyone, it's a pleasure to see you again. Brothers of my soul," Yuri said with a little more strength in her neck and stomach. "First of all, I would like to make it clear that I am not coming back to join the Red Wind Brotherhood."

The men in the room managed to hold back their words and concentrate on her voice.

"As you all know, I left the Brotherhood four years ago and committed myself to the Discarded. I am here as an ambassador for Joshua Kwon. I—no, Joshua and all the Discarded need the Brotherhood. We are going to start a full-fledged war with the Alliance government. Brothers, I still remember the Day of Disaster. I don't think you've forgotten either."

A few people expressed their sympathy in low voices.

"We people of Valhalla have always been a thorn in the eyes of the Alliance, because we have never completely succumbed to them. We have never done any injustice to them, but what have they done to us? What did they do to our parents and brothers, friends and children, for the reason that we have declined to join them?"

Karan Shetty stopped laughing and looked at her.

Yuri accepted those eyes as they were and said, "That's why we formed the Brotherhood. The members of the Red Wind Brotherhood are the best warriors in the star system, if not the whole world of mankind. I'm here because I need warriors. Do you want to defeat our oppressors? It's time to put a mace on Amon Soros and the unscrupulous administration. Come and fight with me. We have to fight.

It may be difficult alone. We have Root Restorationists. They are united like us against the Alliance that has taken away their name and roots and destroyed their lives. They are with Discarded too"

Karan's men nodded and muttered to each other. Yuri felt the atmosphere in the room gradually rise.

"It sounds like you want to make Valhalla into Han, Yuri Ivanova?" said Theresia.

The men stopped talking and looked at him.

"You're putting us in limbo," he said. "No one knows what the Mining Guild on planet Han looks like now. And people say it was just because of an accidental alien attack? No, the Planetary Union government was involved. I remember the overwhelming power they showed us that day. The Valhallan autonomous government failed to resist them and was crushed. Why are you so convinced we can take down Amon Soros and his army? We need a more convincing reason to put our lives on the line for this, for an uncertain victory, if we're going to be working with disgruntled people like you."

Gain said with a smirk. "Theresia, do you know that you're insulting your brothers right now? It's you who makes us look like cowards."

Karan Shetty raised a hand to cover Gain's mouth. When Gain sent him a look of protest, Karan shook his head with a cold expression, as if to say, *Wait.*

Yuri looked around at the people gathered in the room. Warriors with female names. Everyone was waiting for her answer. She counted to three in her mind. Then, after contemplating once more whether she should tell them this or not, she opened her mouth.

"There are those who will help us, the Diutinians."

The last of Karan Shetty's cigarettes burned out.

When the meeting ended and only the two of them were left, Karan Shetty said, "You didn't want to say those last words, did you?"

Yuri, who was sitting on a chair with her eyes closed, opened her eyes and looked at him.

"Is that really true? Diutin will help us?"

Yuri looked down at her feet.

He watched her closely. "You're not sure, are you? You talked to my men as if it were the truth to entice me. But it was all a lie."

"Karan."

"That's right." Karan Shetty nodded. "I thought so. I should've known, given your sudden arrival here. Joshua Kwon didn't even send a message directly."

"Communications are easy to intercept."

"There's a way to contact you anyway, Yuri. Where's your boss?"

"The Adola planetary system. It's a part of the Diutin Federation."

Karan's eyebrows rose in surprise. "What? Why is he there?"

She gave a wry smile. "It's nice to see you startled. I'm not totally lying, Karan. Captain Joshua has been summoned to the Diutin Council. I don't know yet what they have in store for us." She shook her head, lost in a memory. "It was so crazy when the Diutinians showed up in Altra and took the *Robespierre*. Captain Joshua will try to get their help this time. I'm sure of it."

Karan sat down on the mahogany chair. "So, the rumors that the Discarded attacked the Confederacy's capital are true."

"Yes. I was there."

Karan let out a loud, hoarse laugh. "I like you because you're bold."

"You still like me? I left you four years ago and haven't spoken to you since."

Karan's eyes met Yuri's. He stood up and approached her. The top of his shirt was unbuttoned as he leaned over her lap. "It's not too late now. We can go back to that time."

Yuri shook her head, putting a hand on his chest to hold him back. "I'm not interested in that right now, Karan. All the attention I give you is focused on the revolution."

"You'll want me again soon, Yuri Ivanova. I promise," he murmured.

The most famous space pirate in the system straightened, buttoned his shirt, and walked to the door.

"Where are you going?" asked Yuri.

"I'm going to drive for a while. Take a break, Yuri. You don't have to go right now, do you?"

"I'm leaving tomorrow. Give me an answer by then, Karan."

"Okay. Let's talk again tomorrow. I've told my subordinates to reserve a room for you."

With that, he was gone.

Yuri thought of Danny Carlos. The telekinesis powerhouse who once stole her heart.

Seeing Gain on the watchtower, Jena called out, "What are you doing up there?"

"Jena, are you the dawn watchman?"

"Surveillance is not my job; it's the detector's."

The photon detector picked up the location of objects that reacted by emitting light. It was watching and monitoring Valhalla and the movement of the Allied forces in the Behemoth planetary system. The photon detector was perhaps the most important piece of equipment to protect the Brotherhood.

Gain put his rifle down near the detector and sat down on one of the chairs atop the watchtower, as Jena climbed up to join him. "You don't seem very surprised," said Gain.

"Why should I be surprised?" asked Jena.

"She's back. Wasn't it nice?"

Jena shrugged. "It was a little fun."

"I knew she would come back someday. The wind is bound to return to the plateau again, isn't it?"

Jena sat down on the other chair and closed his eyes without answering.

"It's been four years, but she hasn't changed," said Gain. "She was confident and didn't hesitate to express her thoughts. It seems that she has matured after seeing so much out there in the star system. I don't think I'm the only one who was happy to see her. Why did Theresia push her like that?"

"He's terrifying," said Jena. "And he's only speaking for the more cautious people. Don't hate him too much."

"It's not that I hate him. It's just sad."

"There will be many opinions among those in the Brotherhood. The role of Theresia earlier was to express those opinions. It is important that his concerns are shared and not ignored." Jena opened his eyes.

Gain thought carefully about Jena's words.

"Did you see how many of the men shuddered when she brought up the Day of Disaster?" Jena continued. "That was smart of her. I think she'll get what she wants, if she keeps talking that way."

"What do you think of her proposal?" asked Gain.

"I don't know yet. But…"

"But?"

Jena looked at the plateau and thought of the old Yuri. A child who still had hopes for the future. "I have no idea which way the proposal will lead us."

"Is that so? I believe in Yuri Ivanova."

"We are pirates, Gain. No matter what we do, that fact won't change. All we have to do is attack whoever the captain wants us to attack and capture their ship. Whatever Yuri Ivanova suggests, I don't care if the captain accepts it."

Gain noticed a hover bike speeding down the plateau.

"Is that Yuri?" asked Jena.

"It's the captain's hover bike." Gain frowned. "Where's he going at this hour?"

Jena watched as Karan's bike moved away.

Karan raced across the Balthazar Plateau.

The wind strongly pushed the body of the bike. It felt like it was going to rip through the wind like a knife. A herd of cattle was moving in the distance. The cows lined up at the bottom of the ridge were grazing on the pasture in the morning light. They looked like dots in a landscape painting.

Karan thought of the man the plateau was named after. Balthazar Mayer. He was aboard *James Cook* when the four migrant ships from the original solar system arrived in the Desirée star system. He was the leader of a gang from Central America, known as the "one-armed Balthazar" in his hometown.

James Cook's passengers made their roots in the planetary system closest to Earth on the galactic map of the three planetary systems that made up the Desirée. It was a system now called the Behemoth, after the red giant that cast its light upon Valhalla. Three other rocky planets and one gaseous planet orbited the Behemoth star, including the rich terrestrial planet the *James Cook* settlers first landed on, New Sydney.

They were 200 light-years from Earth. Balthazar described in his autobiography that when he arrived in New Sydney, he felt like a Robinson Crusoe in outer space, dropped into a world no one knew about. New Sydney was a world covered in green, ready for them to farm, build temples, create gods, form tribes, and live again as a new human race.

But conflict soon started between the migrants who settled in the southern and eastern hemispheres of New Sydney. Exactly twenty-five years after *James Cook* landed on New Sydney, the conflict escalated into warfare between the South and the East.

Balthazar, who belonged to the relatively sparsely populated East, raided the South by controlling his men with the gang techniques he had learned on Earth. Through their assassinations and kidnappings, guerrilla warfare, and piracy in the New Sydney Ocean, they gradually brought the balance of war upon them. Balthazar thought that victory had passed to him. But he was unaware that not only the settlers of the South, but also the people of the East, wanted to end the damn war.

The South and East united into one political body, and Balthazar became a discord in New Sydney.

Rebelling, Balthazar Mayer, along with thousands of his followers, settled on the twin rock planet, coordinates Q-4. He named it the "Hall of Warriors," or Valhalla.

Karan thought about how Balthazar must have felt when he settled on this sand planet. How this earth, resembling New Sydney but with its extreme barrenness, would have seemed to him. A land of opportunity? Or the land of the exiles displaced by their affluent brethren?

Balthazar had been a rogue with a heart full of anger. History was run by such rogues.

Karan knew that the version he was considering was low-probability and high-risk. He knew it as soon as Yuri Ivanova delivered Joshua Kwon's message. Nevertheless, a part of this gamble was churning in Karan's mind. He wondered what would be at the end of that uncertainty.

Most of all, Karan liked the fact that the uncertain and dangerous game might destroy him.

He was descended from the pioneer Balthazar, and was the worst pirate in the system.

Karan Shetty smiled with a contorted face and sped up his hover bike.

The dust rose in a mess.

At one end of the plateau were neatly arranged tombs. Lonely graves that few people visited. Yuri saw a man standing there.

"Theresia."

Theresia turned to look at her and then looked back at the tomb.

"How did you get here, Yuri?"

Instead of answering the question, Yuri asked one of her own. "Are you still managing the grave? It's in good shape.

"If we don't take care of it, it'll be forgotten. These aren't graves that can be forgotten like that."

"Are there any recently added graves?"

Theresia looked at her. Yuri read the pain on his face.

"Tombs are still being added, Yuri. And I think maybe you will make more tombs."

"Is Julia's grave here?"

Theresia raised his hand and pointed to one side. Yuri's gaze followed his finger to a well-kept grave, with no weeds growing around it.

Dear Julia, sleep here.

Yuri approached the tomb, put her hands together, and bowed her head.

Theresia came behind her and revealed a necklace from his pocket. A faded gold necklace. Yuri knew that the owner of the necklace was Julia.

"Don't think that everyone who has lost a loved one will want revenge, Yuri. There are many who hope that no disaster will ever happen again."

Yuri straightens. "My suggestions are to avoid a terrible future in which your brothers will be forever subordinated, Theresia. Have you ever thought of that?"

"And what if it's not subordination, but a future in which we all perish? Maybe subordination is better. I don't know yet."

Theresia lifted the bottle in his hand, took the lid off, and splashed water on the headstone of the tomb in front of Yuri.

"I hope you know what war with the Alliance means," he said. "Many people on this planet still remember the moment when thy took over the planet."

"Karan will make a decision soon."

Theresia laughed. "I know very well. And if the captain says he'll do it, if he decides to do it…we'll do it together. That's what it means to be brothers."

It was the next morning when Karan returned, covered in dust from speeding through the dawn on his bike. He summoned his men without changing his clothes.

When Yuri entered the conference hall, dozens of subordinates had gathered. Karan glanced at her and said, "Listen, brethren. The Red Wind is at war with the Planetary Union Government."

A sigh broke out. It was a sound close to a moan. Theresia stepped forward from the murmuring crowd and said, "Captain. Has it already been decided?"

"Yes."

"Okay."

After that, Theresia said no more. Yuri was not surprised he'd agreed so easily, but the other brothers were. They muttered to each other, their brows furrowed.

Karan Shetty continued with a calm expression, "I know everyone has different ideas. I won't listen today. My thoughts are firm. We fight the Union and we will win it. On the day of disaster, our fathers were defeated by the Union government. Subjugation has been rampant in the homeland of the warriors. We must fight to break this bondage."

He paused for a moment and stared at the crowd with a beastly expression on his face.

"Above all else, we are pirates. Who said the sons of wind are weak? I intend to collect the blood from the Union government. And that blood price must be greater than anything we've ever done."

Yuri felt the heat radiating from the bodies of the men gathered in the conference hall.

"What the hell do you mean?" said Judy.

Karan looked at Judy. "New Sydney."

The men were quiet. They pondered Karan's words for a moment, reflecting on their meaning.

New Sydney? At first, they were perplexed. But their captain's expression was serious. Their confusion gradually shifted into enthusiasm.

From somewhere a short, thick cry rang out. Soon, all over the place, the men began to chant Karan's name.

"Karan! Karan!"

Karan Shetty enjoyed the cheering with a look of ecstasy.

"Comrade Ivanova," he said. "Guide us to Joshua and

his fleet. And tell him the Red Wind is willing to help the Discarded. In return, you must give me New Sydney."

Yuri felt dizzy as she nodded. *Joshua, I told you not to take the men of my hometown lightly.*

Everyone gathered there was only watching Karan's mouth.

"Jena, prepare all the ships for departure. We need to clean up Valhalla first."

"Where's your destination, Captain?" Jena asked in a calm voice.

"The Valhalla Mobile Flyer."

The first battle began on the barren planet.

4.

Danny Carlos frowned for a moment as he entered the Hao Wei pub on the western outskirts of Dead Dogs Street. The smell of bitterness pierced his nose.

The dirty pub was packed with people. Pimp old women, drug dealers, rapists, third-rate gang members, unidentified women with guns, and the worst humans the pioneer planet Ganesh could create came together to create a trio of noise, disorder and crime.

Danny took a seat in a corner of the bar and ordered from the bartender. "Any single malt whiskey."

The female bartender, with her hair tied back, nodded and disappeared. After a while, she brought a glass and set it down in front of him.

"Thank you."

He downed the glass and soon felt the intoxication rising. After days of suffering, his body screamed and his head hurt.

"Drink slow, Danny," said the person sitting next to

him. "How are you going to keep up if you drink that fast?"

Danny looked and saw the person next to him was Aiden, a member of the Third Regiment who had been dispatched to Ganesh with him. Aiden called the bartender and ordered a whiskey.

"I thought you were at work today," said Danny.

Aiden frowned. "I switched with Lu Xun. Jenny is sick. I've heard that you're coming here these days. What's wrong with you?"

"Your daughter? Where does it hurt?"

"She caught a cold. It's not a big pain, but whenever she says she's sick, my heart sinks. Especially these days."

"It's because you're married. Singles like me have nothing to fear."

"Don't lie, Danny. I don't think you're going to be single all your life."

Aiden lowered his voice.

"Have you heard anything from her?"

"Who?"

"You know…your woman."

"Stop saying bullshit, Aiden. She's a Discarded. How can I meet a traitor?"

"It's really boring today, Danny. I mean, everyone in the world knows when I know you don't care about that."

Danny glanced at the crowd gathered inside the pub. "The truth is, Aiden. I don't have time to think about Yuri Ivanova these days. They're my biggest concern right now." He pointed to a corner of the room, where a group of men and women with short hair were sitting.

"Who are they?" asked Aiden.

"They said, 'A meeting for liberation from oppression.'"

"Oh, you're on duty, Danny? I didn't know that."

"These days, I often get very confused as to whether I'm working or not. I haven't submitted for overtime yet."

"Danny, don't overdo it. Take some time off."

"I've been watching them for a few weeks. "They're part of the Root Restorationists. They definitely know Jinsoo Kim."

"You were on vacation too long. Is this your grandfather's order?"

"That's right. I'm on dispatch for a while."

"I'll give you one piece of advice, Danny. If I were you, I'd leave here and go to the sauna. Put on a fresh pair of clothes. Recharge and then come back. You'll feel brand-new."

Danny smiled at Aiden. "Thanks for the advice, Aiden. Next time, I'll change my underwear on time." He got up from his chair. "Can I talk with those guys about good hygiene?"

"Danny, don't. If you're not careful, you're going to mess things up. You don't want them to disappear, do you?"

Danny thought of the missing Yuri Ivanova.

"Yeah, right."

He sat down again.

Danny's grandfather, Commander Harry Carlos, ordered his grandson to continue to monitor the hideouts where elements of the Discarded were gathered.

"Something is going to happen soon, Danny. It's the eve of the storm."

Danny wondered if the storm was Harry's or if he meant the storm that was coming to New Shanghai and the Desirée system. Harry was good at hiding his feelings.

"The Roots will rise up soon," he told Danny. "They're

only looking for opportunities. They're going to throw the Desirée system into chaos and return to the Earth they want so much. They're like a swarm of grasshoppers. They never leave anything behind."

Harry didn't say anything about Uncle Yeonsu. It had been over a month since he'd disappeared.

But Danny knew. The fact that Yeonsu Carlos had disappeared along with Karl Ryoma, the head of the Root Restorationists. It had happened right after Joshua Kwon, who was driving the *Robespierre*, attacked Altra, along with Karl and his retro-revolutionary followers. Karl and his supporters were imprisoned, but they had escaped, and rumors continued to circulate that it was Yeonsu who helped them.

To make things worse, the Allied secret project ship *Admiral Cheng Ho*, which was sleeping in the Alliance Research Institute, had disappeared. A ship that had finally realized the long-cherished dream of mankind, faster-than-light or warp-drive technology.

Danny was sure that Karl Ryoma was headed to Earth.

He wondered, though, why his grandfather didn't say anything about the missing Yeonsu. Something must have happened between them.

It rained on the gloomy buildings of Ganesh City.

It had been over two weeks since Danny scoured Hao Wei's pubs and streets. He'd met all different types of humans. Most of them were backstreet people who didn't have a Social Security registration certificate. Residents of Ganesh feared the officials of the Planetary Union government. They seemed to think that the government officials would deprive them of the few benefits of their lives. Danny looked at them and thought of wild dogs.

The inhabitants of Ganesh had different names than Danny was used to. Their names were all surnames and names on Earth, the hometown of their ancestors, as if they were randomly sewn together. Sakai Muhammad, Ahyoung Shen, Ishbat Vlador, etc. Most had surnames randomly assigned by the Union government after the First Name War. The surnames were picked by the government's naming machine from numerous cultures in the mother district. After the Second Name War, there were some who paid a certain amount of tax and changed their last name, but such people were few. The more places where there were such people who had not changed their last name, the more unstable the security and the higher the probability was that unfavorable forces were living there. Socialists, separatists, drug lords, Discarded, criminal gangs, idiots, pimps.

Settled in New Shanghai of the planetary system of Shennong, the *Fuxi* ship had been built in Shanghai, the city of the mother district. While 60 percent of the crew were Chinese, the remaining 40 percent were from various countries that helped build the ship. This was also the case with the three migrant ships of Korea's *Hwanung*, Japan's *Amaterasu*, and Australia's *James Cook*. Although the proportions were different, the four migrant fleets from East Asia and the Pacific were multinational ships that contained the wishes of many countries on Earth.

Ganesh Sharma, who pioneered the planet Ganesh, was a geologist aboard the *Fuxi*. Ganesh was a British Indian sponsored by the Indian government. He predicted explosive population growth during the first generation of pioneers in New Shanghai and advocated the development of another planet in the system, a planet full of swamps and mud. Ganesh went directly to the nameless planet, which was called only by its coordinates at the time. He left a research data and wrote various methodologies for terraforming the planet. Ganesh's wish was not fulfilled during his lifetime.

However, more than 100 years after his death, when the government stably entered the planet and established a migration plan in earnest, Ganeshi's research was very helpful. The swamp planet was rapidly terraformed. The plan was based on the cultivation and oxygenation of certain mosses that inhabited mainly swampy areas. The New Shanghai government named the planet "Ganesh."

Danny wondered what Ganesh would think of his planet now that it had become a hotbed of endless slums and crime. He was back in the same pub as before, drinking like before. This time there was only one of the short-haired men in the pub.

The man smiled at Danny, then came to his seat and said to the bartender, "Two glasses of single malt whiskey. I'll buy one for this guy." Now that the man was closer to him, Danny realized he wasn't a man at all, but a woman.

The female bartender nodded, as always. After a while, the drink came out. Danny nodded his head slightly.

"Thank you."

"No worries. Aren't you Danny Carlos?"

Danny silently cursed himself for his stupidity. *What gave it away?*

"So, are you?" asked the woman. "My name is Ari." She laughed softly. "It's not an adult name."

Danny raised a glass of wine. "That's a cool name."

"Can I sit next to you?"

"It doesn't matter."

Ari sat down next to Danny.

Danny shook his glass and said, "I thought everyone forgot by now, but I guess not."

"Of course not. It's not easy to forget the Gloomy Joe case. Nice to meet you."

Danny frowned. "It wasn't a very pleasant experience for me personally."

"Oh, I guess I shouldn't have talked about it."

"No. You also bought alcohol. It's okay. You can ask me anything." Danny didn't want to miss this opportunity to get information.

"Was it difficult to subdue him?"

"He was a lot stronger than I realized. I struggled a lot."

"Is it true that he killed over 1,000 people there?"

"It was 1,492 to be exact. It was the weekend and there were more customers than usual."

When twenty-year-old Danny had been sent to a shopping center outside of Connecticut in New Sydney two years ago, Joe Milligan had already killed many. The outer wall of the shopping center was severely cracked, so it was not unusual for it to collapse at any time. Amid the piles of corpses, Joe had a bewildered expression on his face. Danny knew Joe from the military academy in New Shanghai, and even though it didn't fit the situation at all, he approached him and said, "Hey, Joe. How are you?"

They always greeted each other that way.

Joe spread his palms toward Danny, looked at him, sighed, and lowered his hands.

"Hey, Danny. Damn it. Not good. I killed them all.

"Looks like it. Are you okay?"

"I'm not okay, Danny. This isn't okay at all."

"Why did you do this?"

"It's not what I wanted. Absolutely. It wasn't. I heard a voice. And when I woke up, people were all dead."

"Did you hear something?"

"I heard a sound. You know it, Danny. I can't stop when I hear it. They screamed for help. To save them, I had to kill them first.

"Right."

"Danny."

"Huh?"

"You know that, right?"

Danny nodded. "I understand."

There was a constant rattling noise from the building. Danny knew it was going to collapse soon. He looked around with an anxious expression and said, "Hey…what are we going to do now?

Joe chuckled. "Isn't the real question, what are you going to do? Catch me or kill me? The superiors must have given you orders."

"That's right. Their instructions are clear: one of us must not be alive." Danny sighed. "Come with me. I'll try something."

"You want us to leave here together? What do you think I'll be like? Huh? Danny, such an ending doesn't exist or can't exist in the first place."

"Come on, Joe—"

"I'm not going."

"Have you decided?"

Joe looked down at his bloodstained hands without saying a word for a moment. When he lifted his head and looked at Danny, Danny read his will in Joe's eyes.

Now, Danny returned to the reality of the pub with a

bitter expression on his face.

"Was he a scary person before that happened?" asked Ari, the woman with short hair.

"Was Joe? No, he wasn't. He wasn't a person who could easily kill anyone. In fact, he was the opposite—a man with an overly sensitive mind. He was a good man."

Danny didn't say any more about it. He couldn't tell anyone that his powers had become imperfect, and that he, too, sometimes felt out of control. That he, who was an elite telekinetic agent of the Union, at some point had begun to question all of this.

"Ari, if it's okay with you, tell me about you," Danny said before taking a sip of his drink.

Ari smiled at him. "I don't have much to say. My great-grandfather was descended from pioneers. Not people born through artificial insemination, but real pioneers who came here hundreds of years ago. But where is it easy to live? Human has struggled throughout history with having limited food and shelter. So did our great-grandfathers, grandfathers, and fathers. Our great-grandfathers were descendants of pioneers, but their names were taken away by the Union government. Computer-assigned dwellings and names. They came to this swamp planet in search of a new world, but eventually Ganesh was incorporated into the Union, and a life that was no different from that of any other lower class of the Union was passed on to their descendants." Ari laughed. "Now you see that kind of life. This pub here is the legacy my father left for his daughter."

"Oh, you're the owner."

"It's my father's only property left. I don't even remember his face. He left the house when I was a baby."

Danny felt a deep affinity for her. He asked her for

another drink, and she obliged.

"Isn't life like that?" he said. "You only know where you're going after it's gone. There's no such thing as a predictable course."

Ari banged his glass with her own. "A toast among sailors whose destination is unknown."

Danny had a clue. One of his sources—a man who kept twitching unless he was on narcotic drugs—gave him a place for a rendezvous with the Root Restorationists. Danny initially doubted whether he could trust the man. But the name the man put on his lips moved him, because the name of the meeting was "Liberation from Oppression."

The location was another old bar at the end of Dead Dogs Street. The building was three stories high, but from the outside, it looked like a haunted house that was about to collapse. The outside of the building was surrounded by a fence with a no-access sign.

As he entered the building, a man stopped him. "Who are you?"

"Yeonsu Yasuhiro. I was invited."

"I've never heard of such a name."

"You'll hear it often soon. I come from planet Han. He taught me this at Hao Wei Pub."

Danny showed the forged ID card and followed it with the unique way of greeting of the Root Restorationists. He thrust his left fist down in front of his chest.

The man gave him a favorable expression. "You came from there. I'm sorry I didn't know you. I'm particularly sensitive to security these days. Please go inside. The banquet hall is on the second floor."

Danny said thanks and climbed the revolving stairs

to the second floor. He went up the stairs, through the hallway, and past a few rooms. The large, unpainted door opened slightly, and light streamed through the crack. Danny heard the growing noise of voices.

"…By the way, this is your last chance."

About 1,000 men and women were gathered in the large hall. Danny sneaked into the back row, but no one was looking at him. He raised his neck, trying to look at the podium. On the podium, a skinny man was moving around quickly, making eye contact with the crowd at the bottom of the podium.

The person on the podium was Jinsoo Kim, the man he'd been looking for. A separatist and a core henchman of Karl Ryoma. Danny's heart started pounding.

"This is your last chance," Jinsoo Kim said again. "Your last chance to break free from their oppression. Don't miss it. If you miss this time, it will be a long way off the bridle of you and your children. Am I right?"

The crowd responded with a cry of, "Yes!"

Danny spotted Ari in the front row. She was listening to Jinsoo Kim with a passionate expression. It felt like a religious group meeting. Danny chuckled.

But Danny couldn't laugh at Jinsoo Kim's next words.

"Ganesh Municipality has agreed to cooperate with us. The attack on the ground will be led by us Root Restorationists, but the attack from the air and space will be supported by the Discarded and the Ganesh Municipality."

Danny's palms sweat. *Grandfather.* He thought of Harry. This was not just a riot and an uprising. It was a revolt. The crowd roared. The air in the hall was getting dangerous. The mob gathered here shouted and screamed like crazy.

"Kill the oppressors!"

"Kill them!"

"Punish Amon Soros and his unscrupulous government!"

They shouted that they would slaughter the President of the Union government.

Jinsoo Kim exclaimed, "Death to the oppressors!"

The cheers of the enthusiastic crowd drove Danny away. He turned around and left the hall. The Ganesh autonomous government was planning to commit treason. He had to report everything he'd just heard to the Alliance Command.

The man at the entrance of the building looked at Danny in surprise. "Are you done already?"

"It's almost like that." Danny sighed in reply and sprinted out the door.

"Hey," the man called, but Danny didn't look back.

He went to the back alley rather than the main road to avoid being seen. The roads were unpaved and winding. It rained, and the mud splattered and messed up his clothes. But Danny didn't care. He tried to communicate through the handy tool mounted on his wrist, but couldn't pick up a signal. Danny wondered if the infrastructure in this area was inherently poor, or if someone was interfering with communication.

A voice behind him shouted, "Yeonsu Yasuhiro!"

Danny stopped. Looking back, he saw the guard from the meeting place approaching him from the street parallel to the alley. A bigger man appeared behind him. They both held pulse rifles.

"Why are you in such a hurry?" asked the bulky man. "It must have been a meeting you wanted to attend."

Danny spoke smoothly. "I forgot I had an appointment.

But who are you?"

"You know me. You've been spying on me."

"I don't know what you mean. I just happened to see the meeting."

Bulky Man smiled. "Yeah? So, you don't know this guy?

Short Hair came out from behind him.

"Ari," said Danny, his stomach dipping.

Ari laughed. "It's good to see you again."

"Are you a Root person too? It's been so many years, and you don't even know what your roots are?"

"I don't care about my roots. I want to create a world where I can see where my life is going."

Danny looked at her silently and shook his head. "Just for that, you would shed the blood of thousands?"

"Danny, you don't understand, and you never will. You're not like me," Ari said coldly.

Danny shut his mouth. He thought of Yuri and laughed bitterly at himself. *Women are always fucking me. But at the end of the day, they'll say that I don't understand them. Danny Carlos, you really haven't changed.*

The guard walked over and aimed at him.

"We never invite strangers. Ari knows you, Mr. Connecticut Hero. In fact, we knew you were here."

Danny had fallen into a trap.

"Are you going to die here, or will you quietly follow us?"

Danny reached out toward them without answering.

He heard the sound of something breaking in his head. It seemed to be the right side of his brain.

A massive pulse rifle floated up, collided with the other, and exploded.

Ari exclaimed, "Careful!"

She moved her hand to her waist. But she could no longer move her hand. The bulky man called her.

"Ari!"

Sweat dripped down Ari's forehead. Her hand trembled as she was about to pick up the gun around her waist.

Danny opened his mouth. "You'd better not pick up that gun, Ari. And you too," he added to the other men, "or I'll make your brain boil."

The bulky man rolled his eyes. The man who was monitoring the entrance also realized his situation and did not take any action. Ari kept staring at Danny, but she didn't move. Danny foresaw his victory. He narrowed his eyes, trying to knock them out by shocking their brains.

And then the world went haywire.

Danny felt his body slam into a pole by the side of the road. He felt a warm sensation in his hair. Blood. He slid off the pole and fell to the floor.

Before he lost consciousness, he saw a man walking toward him from a distance.

It was Jinsoo Kim.

5.

When Danny opened his eyes, he found himself locked in a cage. The back of his head still throbbed, and he could taste blood in his mouth. The joints all over his body hurt. *Damn it.* He didn't know how he was going to get out of this.

The iron bars looked sturdy, but they were multi-locked with carbon alloy so they could not be broken by his telekinesis. In addition, current was flowing.

The iron door in the hallway outside the iron cage opened, and a man entered. It was Jinsoo Kim. He sat down on the chair with the iron bars in between.

Jinsoo said, "Good morning?"

"…I'm not very good."

"It seems so. I know this place is a bit shabby. Like the Union government, we also suffer from a chronic lack of budget. Still, it's better than sleeping outside. It doesn't look much different, but at least this is a place provided by the Ganesh municipal government."

Danny watched him silently and said, "You're Jinsoo Kim."

"Yes, that's correct. Though actually, my true name is Kim Jinsoo. Of course, it was the Union government that prevented me from putting my last name in front. Back on Mother Earth, we originally put our surnames first and our first names after. Your naming convention is the opposite."

"I thought so." Danny looked around. "Is this the Ganesh government detention facility?"

"That's right. It's a place for fracks like you, Danny Carlos."

Danny noticed that the handy tool attached to his left arm was missing. "Did you take my handy tool?"

Jinsoo ignored his question. "I've been quite curious about you. I've heard of the Connecticut savior many times. It was a heroic act."

"Thanks for the compliment."

"It's nothing. But how did you get telekinesis? You're not from my hometown."

"Not all telekinetic powers are from one planet."

"I know. But all telekinetic powers have something to do with the alien encounter that took place on planet Han twenty years ago. It was then that telekinetic powers were created in human genes. There were many victims that day, hence why there are so many talented people. Of course, some Allied soldiers were also dispatched at that time."

"My father was a telekinetic man," said Danny. "He was dispatched to planet Han during the Big Crush incident. He died shortly after his return."

"It was a telekinetic aftermath?"

"They said so."

"I'm sorry. This is serious."

Danny recalled the sight he had seen before fainting.

"Are you the one who stunned me? Do you also possess a telekinetic talent, Jinsoo Kim?"

Jinsoo nodded. "Yeah. If I was wrong, I could have lost three of my precious crewmembers to you. So, how are you? From what you've seen and heard, do you think we will do well?"

"Why are you asking me that? You're doing a good job on your own, aren't you? Besides, the Ganesh government is also cooperating with you. How are you keeping in touch with Karl Ryoma? How is he giving you instructions to carry out a revolution when he's so far away?"

"You think I'm acting on his orders?" Jinsoo laughed out loud.

Danny's brow creased. "What do you mean? Isn't Karl Ryoma your leader?"

"Ah, that's what most people think. You're half right and half wrong. As your allies, know this: Karl is on Earth right now. You know it's 200 light-years from Earth to the Desirée system, right? Even if they want to send a radiowave to us, it's a distance of 200 years. Danny, even if the warp-drive engine actually exists, and we might be able to get there, we haven't overcome the limits of communication yet."

"Does that mean…the movement of the Restoration sects in the Desirée system is independent of Karl Ryoma?"

"It's not like that. Karl knows we're going to start a war soon. That's what we discussed before he left. But the Restorationists of the star system are now listening to my orders," Jinsoo said. "Karl is my precious friend. And the idea of restoring our roots is something we both created together."

Danny felt like he had been hit in the back of the head. "You were the head."

"That's right. Congratulations. Correct answer."

"Why are you telling me this? And why didn't you kill me? It seems like there's something on your mind."

Jinsoo clapped his hands. "Your head is doing well. Yeah. Actually, I'm very happy right now. I was going to kill you myself because I thought you were a spy, but now I'm quite sure we're lucky to have someone like you."

"Are you going to use me as a hostage?"

"Something like that. You're the only blood of Commander Harry Carlos. Your presence here will be a very heavy burden on Harry Carlos when we start a full-fledged war with his forces. Or, we can use you as an ambassador. Leaders always prepare for war and negotiations at the same time."

Danny laughed at Jinsoo. His laughter grew louder at Jinsoo's puzzled expression.

"You don't know my grandfather very well. Terrorism, negotiating with a treason group? He won't care what you do to me, or what you use me for. I advise you, Mr. Kim Jinso, it would be better to end this before you make a bloodbath of your people. The size of the Allied forces you'll have to deal with will be formidable."

Jinsoo laughed. "Let's see, Danny. Sometimes people can surprise you." He got up. "Tell me if I can provide anything for you. We don't have a bed, but perhaps something else can make you more comfortable."

Danny didn't say anything. As if Jinsoo didn't want an answer, he left the prison room.

Alone, Danny wondered how long it would take Aiden to find him.

Yuri activated the hologram communication reception function of her handy tool. After a while, a clear connection sound came from the communicator. A hologram appeared on the handy tool. It was a white-haired man with a stout build, the land squadron captain Kamura Park.

"Yuri. Are you on Valhalla?"

"That's right, Kamura."

"How did the deal with the Red Wind go?"

"They've agreed to help us. The attack will start from Valhalla."

"Good. You've done well, Yuri."

Yuri hesitated. "But there is a condition that Karan Shetty put forward. It's a bit tricky."

"Conditions? What did he ask for?"

"After the war, he wants us to give them New Sydney."

Kamura scoffed. "I suppose we should've expected a request like that from a pirate."

"I said I would pass it on to Captain Joshua. Wasp, I think she should know too."

"Yuri, I'm worried. Are we making a deal with more people we can't control?"

"It's already begun, Kamura. And the captain said we need the Red Wind no matter what they ask for. We need them to win this war."

"I hope Captain Joshua made the right choice."

Yuri sighed. "What about the other two planetary systems? Any news from them?"

"Yes, and it's good news. The Ganesh government has also agreed to cooperate with us. He is coordinating with Jinsoo Kim, and soon, according to their plan, we will also send additional attack ships to the Root Restorationists."

"The Ganesh government?" Yuri's eyebrows rose; she was impressed. "This is moving faster than I thought."

"Governor Sakai, the head of the Ganesh' government, seems to think there's a little more left to fall on our side. Ultimately, he wants the Alliance system to collapse and Ganesh to become independent. I don't think he wants it to be semi-independent and subordinate to New Shanghai, as it is now. I don't know if he's a nationalist yet."

"I don't know him exactly, but he had a close relationship with my father. I was very young back then, so I never talked to him. Keep in touch and find out what they want, Kamura."

"Okay."

Many people were fighting the war that was about to begin with different ideals and goals. Yuri didn't know if this was a good thing. Different goals implied that cracks were easy to form.

But one thing was certain: there were countless people who wished for the collapse of the Alliance.

"I have to go back soon. When will I see you?"

"We'll be arriving in Valhalla soon."

"Is there anything wrong with the *Moscow*?"

"It's okay. Everyone is waiting for the captain to come back. Ah, the Haneul has entered the command room, and Junkou has officially reported as a new flight member."

Yuri smiled broadly. "That's great. See you soon, Kamura. I've written a message for Captain Joshua, so please pass it on for me. These are the things I just shared with you."

"Okay, Captain."

Kamura's hologram disappeared.

Kamura ended the communication. He looked over the

message Yuri had sent to him and checked the time. There were still thirty minutes before it was time to communicate with Joshua. He headed to the bridge.

The *Moscow* was a large-class battlecruiser. About 300 crewmembers were on board, led by Captain Yuri Ivanova. Control room personnel looked at Kamura and said hello. Kamura was serving as the interim captain while Yuri was away. He reached the bridge after about ten minutes. As he stood on the bridge, Haneul Bravo saluted him.

"Are you here, Captain?"

"Haneul, I'm the temporary captain. You don't have to salute me so passionately."

"Still, the current commander of the *Moscow* is the captain."

"It's nice to see the spirit in it. Keep it up when the real captain returns."

"I will!"

It was a childish thing, but looking at the Haneul Bravo made him feel good. She was a kid with a straight heart, who was passionate about everything. An elderly soldier, Kamura sometimes recalled his youth when he saw those young kids.

The gates of the bridge opened, and Junkou Meg entered and saluted. "Land Battle Commander, I report the transfer of Junkou Meg."

"Your uniform suits you well, Junkou. You look like an old-timer who has just woken up from pilot life."

Junkou grinned. "Thank you, Captain.

"Did the reconnaissance work?"

"Yes, this place is safe."

"Good job. Go back and rest."

"Okay." He glanced at the Haneul and smiled softly

before he left.

The Haneul was rigid, focused on the screen in front of her.

Kamura smiled, watching her. "Haneul, prepare photon communications and radio communications."

"Yes, Captain."

Haneul began to operate the photon and radio transmitters through the signalmen and control officers. The upper central cover of the *Moscow* opened, and a cone-shaped photon generator was directed into space. Both photons and radio waves were communications that traveled at the speed of light. They were the fastest mediums discovered by mankind to date. Joshua Kwon and the Discarded's flagship, *Robespierre*, were far off in the alien system Adola, 110 light-years away from the Desirée system. However, they could send and receive communication at a fixed time once every 100 or so hours, through a wormhole.

After the *Robespierre* was bombarded by Allied ships at the end of the Altra raid, they had been unable to wormhole warp, because the wormhole generator was broken. Kamura, who had boarded the *Robespierre*, still remembered those frightening moments, when he had feared it was the end for them all.

Then, out of nowhere, the ship of Hypkeranos had appeared in front of *Robespierre*. Hypkeranos made a wormhole, and *Robespierre* and several Allied ships disappeared. They'd emerged on the other side of the wormhole in the Diutin system. But Joshua had asked Hypkeranos to send some of his men back to the Desiree system.

"If we stay here, we can't proceed, Kamura," he'd said. "We'll keep in touch through Diutin's wormhole communicator, so help Yuri with our task."

Thus, Kamura had joined Yuri's ship, *Moscow*, as a land battle commander.

Soon, Diutin's wormhole would open and he would be able to communicate with Joshua once again.

A blue light flickered in the empty space in front of the *Moscow*. Space was distorted until it formed a dark indigo-colored cylinder. The commanders on the bridge of the ship watched silently.

It was a wormhole.

Soon, Haneul Bravo came and said to Kamura, "Captain. Communication has arrived. Shall we project a hologram?"

Kamura nodded, and he projected a hologram generator.

A hologram of Joshua Kwon appeared in the center of the bridge. A familiar voice was heard.

"Are you okay, Kamura?"

Kamura thought for a moment about what to say first.

6.

After the communication with Kamura was over, Joshua fell into his thoughts for a moment. Once he collected himself, he left the communication room and started walking toward his residence.

The communication room was on the fifteenth floor. The communications equipment was linked to Adola's outer orbital space station. The station transmitted all of Adola's radio waves periodically through the wormhole to the Adola worlds. The wormhole toward Desirée was a channel that had been added temporarily at Joshua's request.

Joshua's residence was located on the thirty-fifth floor of the Visitor's Tower. The tower was in the shape of a long cone, so it looked more like a pyramid from Mother Earth that he'd seen in class as a child. However, the tower had a concave shape rather than a sharp point. The walls inside the tower were transparent. Joshua still couldn't fully adapt to the walls. It felt like he would fall to the ground if he stepped through them. But of course, when he reached out his hand, the wall had a hard texture. Joshua was curious about what technology the Diutinians had used to build these structures.

Joshua could see ships moored in a spiral dock outside the wall. One of the spiral arms was anchored to the *Robespierre*.

His ship had been seized by aliens, and Joshua and his crew were staying at the Visitor's Tower. Although the aliens were treating them in a fair and impeccable way, it was clear that they weren't entirely free to do as they pleased.

Joshua got into the elevator. The elevators were also transparent, so you could see outside. He shut his eyes tightly. Within seconds, the elevator door opened on the thirty-fifth floor.

He crossed the hallway to his room and opened the door to see Cassie Ice.

"Joshua."

"Cassie, where is Yuna?"

"She's walking around the garden outside. She doesn't want to come inside the building. She has a lot more to see outside and it's amazing."

"Don't worry about Yuna, our warriors are guarding the place."

Joshua noticed someone else was in the room. An alien. "Hyp."

Hypkeranos lifted the teacup with his long fingers. "Joshua. Did communication with the Desirée system go well?" he asked.

"Yes, I received some updates. This is our business, but I don't think it's a big deal if you hear it."

"That won't be necessary." Hypkeranos waved a hand.

"Human work is human. I think it would be rather pointless for me to hear."

"Okay. Cassie, I'll tell you later."

"Okay, Joshua."

Joshua sat in the empty chair in the room and looked at Hypkeranos. "What's going on, Hyp? Any news for me?"

"How did you know I had news?"

"It's just a feeling. At this point, I think you should have some for me. It's already been a month since we arrived here."

"That's right. The council's decision has been made."

Joshua immediately focused on him, gripping his armrests in concentration. So did Cassie.

Hypkeranos said, "A hearing on this case will be held soon."

Joshua had a hard time hiding his disappointment. "The council's decision is just that they will proceed with the case?"

"Joshua, as I've said before, council decisions take time. It's a long time by human standards, but it's about being prudent. Coordination between representatives from different parts of the galaxy. It's necessary, because they must reach a unanimous agreement. Understand, my friend."

"Hyp, I appreciate your kind's prudence and vigilance. But the Desirée system needs me and my crew and the *Robespierre*. You know? We were doing something important."

"Is it something that involves violence on a massive scale?"

Joshua frowned. "What?"

"Violence on a massive scale, Joshua. Violence that will take the lives of many people. Isn't that what you intend to do to overthrow the government of your star system?"

Joshua shut his mouth. After a while, he spoke in a low voice. "Hyp, you shouldn't talk like that. We're the people who almost perished in the Diutin attack."

Hypkeranos flinched, and Cassie looked nervously between the two of them. The Diutinian supported his head with one hand and shook his head. "I'm sorry, Joshua. I didn't mean to say it that way. I just want you to be aware that if you don't adhere to certain principles as you go about your actions, you might be prone to corruption."

"You've said plenty about this, Hyp. Do you have anything else to say?"

"The hearing is due in a few days. For now, you or some of your crew will be interviewed as a reference. You never know how it will be concluded."

"I've been preparing since the time you and your fleet appeared in New Shanghai a month ago and brought us here, Hyp. What will happen if the trial is finalized and I become the accused? Will it be difficult to return to the Desirée system for a while? How much of a felony is it for our ship to use the wormhole technology without permission? I have no idea."

"It's a big sin, Joshua."

"A great sin?"

"That's what I said. Wormhole technology is a technology that we are forbidden to provide to other races. It is a core technology of our civilization. You could be sentenced to severe punishment."

All sorts of thoughts ran through Joshua's head and then disappeared. The word that came out of his mouth was dull.

"Right."

Hypkeranos stood up to leave. "I'll be in touch soon, Joshua. Think about what I said."

After the Diutinian left, Joshua fell into silence. Cassie walked over to him and stroked his cheek.

"Are you worried?"

"Worried? Cassie, I'm not doing this because I'm afraid of what I'm going to do. I'm worried that I'll be stranded here, helpless."

"I know. You're not a coward. You're so impatient about getting back to the Desirée system because you think the war is going to start soon. You think you should be there, don't you?"

"Damn, I don't understand why these guys are doing these things to me. They say that the warp-drive technology aboard the *Robespierre* is theirs. But we didn't steal it from them. Hypkeranos did us a favor. It's the technology he provided, so he should be responsible for it. And whatever the story, it's absolutely true that tens of millions of our people were slaughtered twenty years ago when the Diutin Federation attacked planet Han. A hearing? A trial? It's not enough to apologize to me. What are they gonna do, tie me up for a month? Cassie, do you understand? We should be in Desirée, not here. Helping Yuri Ivanova and our comrades to fight against the Alliance. We have to start attacking!"

"What did Kamura say? How are things going now?"

"They seem to be going smoothly. Yuri attracted the Red Wind pirates, and under the leadership of the Root Restorationist Jinsoo Kim, the Ganesh municipal government has also joined our partnership."

"If that's true, that's great!"

"But we're supposed to be there, Cassie. We need to be

of some help to them at this critical time. I told my people I'd get the Diutinians to help us. I don't see how that's going to happen now." He pressed his face into his hands.

Cassie patted his head. "Joshua." When he didn't answer, she called his name again.

He looked up at her.

"Let's focus on the positives. So, you sent Kamura to Yuri, yes? The crew knows what you want. They're not children; they can handle this. Do you not trust your colleagues?"

"I get what you're saying, Cass."

"And there's the Wasp, Joshua. You have to trust her to help Yuri."

Joshua was silent for a moment, then said, "Right."

"Look at the reality we face now. The hearing of the Diutin Council will begin soon. We need to prepare for what they might conclude and how we should respond if they call for us to speak in their court."

"I don't know what they'll think of us. They're a race that hunted us like animals decades ago. Even if it was a misunderstanding. Will they recognize us as intelligent beings on an equal footing? Or will they leave me to rot in some prison?"

Cassie saw a glimpse of fear in Joshua's eyes. The fear of failure. He didn't show it often.

"Joshua," she said, "we're going back to Desirée with the *Robespierre* soon. It doesn't matter if we go there alone or with the Diutin's help. If the aliens want to put you in a cage, I'll get you out of jail. I swear it. They won't lock up the Discarded's Joshua Kwon forever."

Her voice grew stronger. "We're going back, and we're going to make the Alliance pay the price they deserve.

They'll wonder in aw, where did these terrible plagues come from? In their dying eyes, we will see the ghosts of the planet Han. Our mothers, fathers, brothers, and sisters, friends and loved ones who died at the hands of the aliens you summoned. We will engrave in our ears the songs of the ghosts and say, 'We have never forgotten you. And we will avenge you.'"

He pondered how he had met such a woman. A precious woman. A companion. Joshua took Cassie's hand and squeezed it.

Cassie laughed. "So, until then, why don't you put your worries aside and go pick up our cute Yuna?"

The warrior Dayweo watched the human girl running around in the garden. The child looked around at Adola's native plants with a curious expression. At least, if Dayweo properly understood human expressions, wonder and curiosity were evident. He was a high-ranking warrior, temporarily tasked with guarding the visitors in the tower.

"Yuna Ice!" someone called.

Dayweo turned his head and saw adult humans coming out of the tower's entrance. He knew those people. Joshua Kwon and Cassie Ice? The captain and lover of a ship that had installed Diutin's wormhole technology without permission. When Dayweo first met them a month ago, he was very wary of them. He still hadn't fully let his guard down yet, but he did feel more relaxed around the humans now.

"Mom!" Yuna tied her hair back and ran to Cassie.

"What's so fun out here? You don't want to come inside?" asked Cassie.

Joshua frowned, looking around the garden. "These

plants… Cassie, are these flowers? They look quite unusual. Yuna, were you looking at these flowers?"

"That's right. Look at this one! The leaves are full of light, but when you get closer, the light comes out. It puts my mind at ease." As Yuna approached one of the flowers in full bloom in the garden, the flower smirked and turned its bud toward her. Soon, light flowed from the petals, gathered in Yuna's hand, and then disappeared.

"How do we know it isn't harmful?" said Cassie, biting her lip.

"It's not poisonous," said Dayweo, walking over.

"May I know what the name of this flower is?" asked Joshua.

"Compel. It means 'calling flower.'"

"Why is it called that?" asked Cassie.

Dayweo looked at her and answered, "Once upon a time, many women wept when Proditor the Prodigal betrayed their people and attacked Adola. Mothers, women who sent their husbands and lovers to war, hoping they would return. They planted this flower. The light embraced by the petals is the tears of women, and their longing for the warriors to return."

"Did the warriors come back?" piped up Yuna.

Dayweo smiled. "Some people returned and some didn't, kid. They were the keepers and warriors of our civilization. Our ancestors planted flowers all over the city to honor those who did not return. What you see now are the flowers planted back then."

Yuna smiled shyly up at the alien warrior with a kind voice.

The tall alien said to Joshua, "I don't know what kind of light you came here looking for. But I wish you good luck."

"Thank you."

Cassie put her hand on Yuna's shoulder. "Come on, let's go in, Yuna. It's dinnertime. It's going to get cold. Let's eat and then I'll brush your hair."

Yuna wanted to stay in the garden longer, but she knew her mother was stubborn. The child looked at Dayweo, waved her hand, and headed to the building with her mother. Joshua followed.

Before he went inside, Joshua turned and looked back at Dayweo. "Thank you again for your kind words, Dayweo."

And Joshua disappeared into the tower.

Dayweo was surprised that Joshua knew his name.

7.

Yuri, wearing windproof goggles and a mask, stood in front of her hover bike when Jena appeared from behind.

"Goodbye, Yuri," he said.

She looked back at him, and he shrugged.

"I'll see you soon."

"You will, Jena. Please tell my sister about me as well."

Jena placed his hand on his waist and looked down at the ground for a moment, rubbing his feet on the sand. "At first, everyone hated you."

Yuri frowned. "What?"

Jena shook his head. "After the war with the Allies, most of the boys in Valhalla were renamed. My original name was Zignak, so that was my name until I was eighteen. My father's name was Bar, so to speak. His last name was Nejid, so my last name was also Nejid. I was Zignac Nejid."

The Valhallans had rejected the surnames randomly assigned by the Union through the naming system. They thought that being a member of the Union meant denying their true origins. It wasn't just the name. Amon Soros, who led the Planetary Union Government, didn't want all the inhabitants of the Union to speak freely. Although the Valhallans were told they had autonomy, in fact, they were discriminated against in terms of tax rates and their other obligations as Union citizens. They saw the surname system for what it really was—an act to confuse their identities and weaken the centripetal force of their society.

The people of Valhalla soon decided they had enough, and rose up against the Union government ten years ago. But the Alliance had no trouble suppressing them.

After the war, the Union government "confiscated" all the surnames of the Valhallan people. That was the price that Valhalla got for becoming a member of the Union.

And it wasn't the end.

"My older brother was taken to the Union's forced labor camp and disappeared," said Jena, his jaw tight. "All I know is that while building an orbital airfield, he was hit by a piece of junk floating in outer space. I never got to see his body. My father died during the war, and I was the only son left. My mother, afraid of losing me, suggested that I change my name to Jena. All the mothers in Valhalla changed their sons' names to girls' names, and gave their newborn boys female names as well. Adult males often changed their names too. When sons were dragged into the Union's labor camp, it meant the death of the rest of the family, so we made it seem as if there were no more Valhallan sons. Since we already didn't have any last names, it was already difficult for the Union to keep track of us. We envied you, though, because you have a first and last name of our own choosing. We hated it all the more because the restrictions of the Union meant nothing to immigrants."

Yuri's father had paid huge taxes to the Union government and was granted a "right to inherit the name." That was why he was Kiliman Ivanov and his daughter could be called Yuri Ivanova. Valhallans were not even allowed a surname, only the task of heavy labor.

Yuri looked at the middle-aged man, who sighed. His mother must have wept as she hugged her son who was named after a girl. What choice did she make to avoid losing her last child? Deleted from the resident registration system through death notification, or changed to a female name. Yuri thought of her own childhood. The hostility and fear she'd faced from some of the people here when she first appeared as a stranger on Valhalla.

"Maybe you felt it too?" asked Jena. "Not all of us liked you. I think it must have been quite difficult for you as a child."

"That's right, Jena," said Yuri softly. "To be honest, it was a pretty tough childhood."

"There were skeptics even when you joined the Red Wind. You did so well, Yuri. I was proud of you. Suddenly, you became a part of the Valhallan line. A few people said that you were pretending to be Valhallan but couldn't hear the wind's song after all." Jena looked directly into Yuri's eyes. "I said fuck those who said that."

She grinned at him. "Yeah?"

He nodded. "I told those bastards to shut up. They didn't even know what to do. If they couldn't close their mouths, I closed them myself. Then they shut their mouths. I had to do it, Yuri. If people really understood you, they wouldn't have said that."

"I appreciate that, Jena."

A smile appeared in Jena's deep eyes. "Yuri, I know

you. And I believe in you. We don't know yet where the beginning of this war will lead us, but it can't be avoided. Maybe the path will be a little painful, but I think it will be worth it in the end. If Yuri Ivanova says so, then I believe it. If Yuri Ivanova has to fight the Union government, then she has to fight it."

Yuri thought about her childhood for a moment. A time when she had to surrender her life to the helpless winds, but also a time when she found her brothers in the Red Wind.

"Jena, thank you. You are right. I have never forsaken my brothers. It will be a glorious day for us to meet at the end of this road."

Yuri hugged Jena. Yuri couldn't help feeling a little embarrassed, and nervous about how much he was trusting her in this. Nevertheless, she was grateful to him.

"Tell your brothers, too. I've never forgotten them," she said as she pulled away.

"I will."

"Where's Karan? I tried to say goodbye, but I don't see everyone."

"Oh, everyone went to work." He smiled meaningfully. "Since we've been resting for so long, now we have to work diligently. Don't you agree?"

"What are you looking at so lost in your thoughts?"

Gajin turned his head at Judy's voice. Judy was wearing a robe and smiling at him.

"I was gauging the size of this place," said Gain. "Have you been here before?"

Judy snorted. "Does a pirate ever come to the spaceport? Of course. Yeah, I've been here many times. My uncle worked at customs."

Gajin looked out of the pressure-resistant tempered glass again.

The Valhalla Medium Orbital Spaceport shone brightly on the dim border between Valhalla's atmosphere and outer space. The guide at the information center said that the width of the airport was three kilometers.

Mid-orbit spaceports were Allied-owned facilities primarily used for ships' stopover and other special purposes. When ships that had to go to another planetary system used Valhalla as a stopover, they would stop at an out-of-atmospheric mid-orbit spaceport instead of landing on the ground to complete maintenance and depart. Landing and anchoring consumed a lot of fuel, after all. Most of the military suppliers also used to go through this spaceport to the ground. It was for double and triple security.

The door to the quarantine station opened, and quarantine officers poured out.

"This is the combined quarantine team," one of them called out. "Everyone, stand in three rows. Please take out your invoice and place the baggage you brought separately in front of the inspection bar on the right."

"Gajin, they came out. Let's go." Judy tapped Gajin on the arm.

Gajin hastily fastened his robes and grabbed the handle of the leather bag sitting next to him. The two joined the procession of people heading into the inspection area.

Each quarantine officer had an inspection machine used to scan the handy tools that people offered as identification. Most of the time, a green light came on at the top of the machine. However, sometimes a red light came on instead, and that person fell into the line for additional investigation under the guidance of the quarantine team. After about ten minutes, the line got shorter, and soon it was their turn.

An elderly-looking quarantine officer stopped Gajin and Judy. "Where are you from?" he asked.

"We're with Tianjin Corporation," said Judy with a smile. "These are the items that will be delivered to the Mobile Combat Team base. I'm Rick, and my friend here is Yoji. Even these days, the quarantine team has a lot of work to do, eh? Is it worth it?"

The quarantine officer grumbled. "Don't be fooled. The volume of goods is increasing, so the work is increasing day by day, but we don't have full staffing. This is really going to kill me."

"That's why it's always the superiors who are the problem. They don't ever seem to get how shorthanded they are and how overworked their employees are."

"Ain't that the truth. Anyway, if you're with Tianjin Corporation, those are military trainers. Are you still making deals with the Allied forces?"

"Credit management and delivery are life," said Gajin, changing the subject to avoid answering the question. He hoped this man was so overworked he wouldn't notice. "I've never had a debt due, so I've never been late. Got a credit rating of 1 based on the central bank's credit rating."

"Good for you. You caught a goose that came out of money."

"I have to work harder."

"Show me the document."

Gajin held up his handy tool to the officer's scanner. His heart was beating fast.

A green light came on at the top of the machine. Gajin

sighed inwardly. The quarantine officer pointed forward. "Come on in."

Gajin and Judy passed the grumbling man and headed into the quarantine sector.

Inside, there were a lot more people. Most of them were vendors doing business with the Union.

Judy spotted a male immigration agent at the check-in booth who was wrestling with people from other companies. Judy pointed to the man, and Gajin nodded. As the two of them went to join the line at the booth, they could hear the agent berating a merchant.

"As I told you already, no. How many times have I said that the document is a document, and the procedure from here on is separate! Take out all the immigration documents, and all the inspection certificates, examination certificates, identification certificates, goods movement certificates, and government merchant certificates. You don't have all of those things? Then go back over there, write an excuse, and apply for additional documents. Then why are you still here? Whether you are homeless at the spaceport or go back to where you were, take care! Prepare your documents carefully! It's your fault that you didn't do it, and it's not something I should have to deal with!"

The merchant muttered something, looking flustered, then walked toward a different line in the back.

Judy approached the agent, who was frowning, and held out their papers.

"You're working hard," he said in a cheery voice. "My name is Rick from Tenjin Corporation. Isn't today really an unlucky day? I've prepared all the necessary documents for the screening."

The agent glanced at him and snatched the paperwork.

Judy knew from the man's nameplate that his name was Marcus. Judy assumed that all the immigration agents were from New Sydney. *Yes, Marcus, take a look. Because there will be nothing to fault. You just need to stamp our papers.*

"There are no flaws in the documents," said Marcus.

Gajin gave him a bright smile.

As he returned the papers to them, Marcus asked, "The purpose of entry is to deliver these supplies to a mobile combat group base?"

"Yes. It's all military supplies. From clothing to small military accessories and parts."

"As you can see, it is a company that supplies periodically every quarter," Gajin said.

Marcus looked at Judy and Gajin in turn. Gajin, who belonged to the relatively young axis, gave off the impression of being slender and delicate among the Valhalla people. Before departing for the mid-orbit spaceport, Karan had told Judy he was sending Gajin with him because, "He doesn't look threatening." Gajin just came to mind with those words.

"Where are the supplies?" asked Marcus.

"Dock 24."

"Usually, all items and ships need to go through inspection…but your company has been dealing with the base for over ten years, and I'm having a bit of a headache right now."

You poor agent, thought Judy. *You have no idea something interesting is about to happen soon that will give you a worse headache.*

Bang bang. Marcus stamped Gajin and Judy's passports, and the documents they brought with them, and shouted, "Next!"

Inside the spherical merchant ship, Karan pressed the button on the handy tool when Judy's communication came in.

"Immigration and customs procedures are complete, Captain."

Karan smiled contentedly. Like a child holding his favorite toy in his hands.

"Wonderful. Now, it's time play. Theresia, let's go. Judy, follow me as soon as you can."

"Aye, Captain."

Theresia's voice came from the cockpit. "Ready to depart, Captain."

The merchant ship, which was moored at Dock 24 at the orbital spaceport, slowly pulled its body backward and began to move away from the dock.

Karan took out the plasma cutter handle hanging from his waist and activated it. Plasma poured out of the handle shaped like a blade, emitting a light source that could blind a person.

Karan held the plasma cutter in his hand and wiggled his legs, immersed in pleasant imaginations.

8.

Desmond Janice, a member of the Valhalla Mobile Combat Team from New Sydney, saw a familiar ship loaded with military supplies arriving at the base at around two o'clock. He informed the command room that a merchant ship belonging to the Tenjin Corporation was approaching the base dock, and the commanding officer on duty allowed the merchant ship to enter the port.

Desmond and the guards on duty headed to the dock to meet the ship. It was a faded dark gray color with the blue paint peeling off the name, *Blue Wagon.*

The warehouse door behind the merchant ship was open. From the inside, about twenty men drove forklifts to transport goods to the outside. Desmond waited quietly for them. After hopping off a forklift, a dark-skinned man with curly black hair came up to him and presented him with a receipt.

"It's cold out here," said the man with a shudder. "It's spring, but it doesn't feel like spring."

"Isn't it? You've worked hard. The company isn't doing much these days, right?"

"Ain't that the truth. I don't have anything interesting to do. Wish something special would happen."

"So do I."

"There may be a lot of interesting things happening soon," said the captain who appeared behind Desmond.

The curly-haired man eyed him and asked Desmond, "Who is this?"

"Ah, this is Captain Hasebe, the new arrival."

"Which planet does Tenjin Corporation belong to?" asked Hasebe.

"The headquarters are in Ganesh," said Desmond. "Most of the shares are owned by a consortium led by a state-owned company in New Shanghai. Well, you can think of it as New Shanghai, not Ganesh. I have a warehouse and my office in New Shanghai."

"Okay." The captain looked at the curly-haired man. "What's your name?"

"My name is Kay, Captain."

"Do you have a surname? It's become a habit to ask for your surname after coming to Valhalla."

Kay didn't say anything for a moment and then smiled. "I'm from Valhalla, Captain. That's why I don't have a surname."

The captain frowned. "You're from Valhalla. How did you get to the Shennong system to join the company?"

"My uncle married a woman in Valhalla. He cared for me a lot, so he often took me to Ganesh and New Shanghai. I didn't get a surname because of the Union Act, which is a shame, but what does it matter? Anyway, thanks to my uncle, I was lucky enough to get a job in Tenjin, and now

I have opened a deal with the Allied base in my mother's hometown."

"You're lucky. But it's important to recognize your roots properly. The fundamentals don't change. Still, congratulations. You've come to live like a human being away from a place full of rotten rats? That's a success to be praised."

Kay didn't like the captain. He made sure to memorize the captain's face in his heart. *A weasel of a man.*

Desmond coughed and looked into Kay's eyes. "Can you move the items to the inner warehouse? And they said that they sent parts and materials for ship repair to your side in a hurry to receive the delivery from the command today. Thank you, Kay."

"I will." He turned and called to the other men. "Hey, did you hear that, everyone? Let's move quickly."

The men drove more than twenty forklifts and, guided by the guards, began to move goods to warehouses and hangars.

Hasebe, who was watching the scene, said to Desmond. "They are trash."

"Excuse me?"

"Not only that man, but most of them are Valhallan. Can you see it, Desmond?"

Desmond observed the drivers driving the forklifts. "I don't know, Captain. How can you tell?"

"I checked all of the inmates who reported to the guardhouse today. That's why I came out here."

"They're not suspicious, Captain. They've been doing business with us for quite some time."

"Next time, think about changing your business partner. Report it officially to headquarters. The Valhallan people are unbelievable. There are many people who still have the memories of the war. There's a reason why the base crew here is only from New Sydney."

Desmond thought about what to say, but kept it to himself. Captain Hasebe was a stubborn man.

"Okay. I'll write a draft. I'll go check on the loading process in the hangar-side warehouse."

"Okay."

Desmond disappeared, and Hasebe looked around the guardhouse for a while. After an hour, he walked toward the site headquarters command room.

In the headquarters command room, the soldiers on the watch were tied up in a seated position with their hands above their heads, disarmed. Hasebe looked at his subordinates with a bewildered expression.

"What are you guys doing?"

"As you can see, I'm quietly meditating, Captain."

Hasebe saw the man standing in the doorway with his arms wide open. It was Kay.

"What?"

As Hasebe placed his hand on his waist, Kay whistled.

"I wouldn't do that. Quit before your wrists fly, Captain."

Hasebe pulled out his pistol. The next moment, his right wrist flew off.

Drops of blood flowed, and Hasebe collapsed, screaming in pain.

Kay looked down at him with the plasma cutter in hand. "I told you not to."

Hasebe was about to pass out from the pain, but he tried to grasp the situation. It wasn't difficult. Because there was only one human in the system who used a plasma cutter to cut everything.

"Karan…Shetty!"

"I'm sorry I couldn't introduce myself properly sooner."

Karan gave him a big grin, and his pirates stormed into the command room.

"Captain, we are taking over the base smoothly," said Theresia.

Karan sent a sign that he understood.

A fire erupted inside the base. Gunshots rang out, and screams pierced the air outside the command room. A part of the building collapsed with the sound of the barrel of the pulse rifle turning.

Hasebe couldn't believe what was happening. "Where the hell did you come from?" And then it hit him. "The cargo delivery!"

"You're quick-witted, Captain," said Karan. "That's right. These guys popped out of the luggage we brought. A cool idea, eh? Won't Balthazar be satisfied when he sees that they're really smart guys?"

Hasebe clenched his teeth. His hands trembled and saliva dribbled out of his mouth. The severe pain in the area where his wrist had been severed felt like he was being stabbed without mercy by a skewer heated with fire.

"Karan Shetty, you are foolish," he spat. "Mobile squadrons and ground forces circling the planet will arrive here soon."

"Yeah, I need to finish this before that. That's why I came to the command room."

Karan was also calculating that much. As long as he gained control of the command room, other army bases on the planet would not be able to know the situation of the task force. However, if the task force did not respond to the call, their game would soon be up. Karan thought they had maybe three or four hours.

He turned on his handy tool. "Desmond. How's it going?"

Desmond's response came through. "Five ships. One large cruiser, two heavy cruisers, and two assault ships. We will board them and take off soon."

"Good."

Hasebe forgot the pain and shouted, "That bastard! How could he have an affair with the human dwarves of Valhalla?"

"Hey, noble captain. Can't you be quiet? That's the fundamental difference between you and me. Whether you're from New Sydney or Valhalla, I'll accept any friend I like. You should really learn to trust people more."

Gajin's voice came through the handy tool comm link. "Captain?"

"Where are you?" asked Karan.

"We're over the base. Their anti-aircraft guns stopped, so it seems we've taken control of the command post."

"Soon Desmond and his brothers will take off with the stolen ships. Prepare for orbital bombardment. Sweep the base."

"Won't that attract too much attention?"

"It doesn't matter. It's better for them to notice and attack. I'm going to destroy them all."

Gajin took a breath. "Got it."

Desmond said, "Captain, the crew still can't handle the ships perfectly."

"Just open the guns and shoot forward. We'll cover the rest."

"Aye, Captain."

After finishing the communication, Karan raised

Hasebe's bloody, writhing hand and waved it in front of his eyes. "Contemplate in heaven what lesson you have learned today from this hand. Goodbye, Captain."

The plasma cutter slashed through the air, and Hasebe's neck was separated. Blood gushed out.

Goodbye, Captain. Hasebe had never imagined that such meaningless words would be the last words he would ever hear in the world. His head looked at his body. A little pain and sadness flooded in. Hasebe's head hit the wall, bounced, and rolled.

His mouth twitched a few times and then stopped.

Desmond grumbled and shouted as he entered the interior of the large cruiser, *Witch Hunter.*

"This ship now belongs to the Red Wind. If you resist, I will kill you!"

The pirates who came in with Desmond aimed their rifles at the control personnel on board.

"Desmond? What's this?" The crew of the ship recognized him and ran to him.

Desmond grinned at them. "Everyone, back down."

The crewmembers were astonished by his betray. Someone shouted, "You motherfucker!"

He moved his hand to his waist, but fell to the ground with a hole in his chest. One of the pirates had shot him. Desmond clicked his tongue.

"Let's not resist needlessly. I don't want to kill you. But if it is absolutely necessary, I will kill you without hesitation."

Everyone went still. The crew looked at each other. Desmond smiled.

"I'll say it one more time. Put down our weapons right

now and gently guide us to the leader of the ship."

Desmond and dozens of armed pirates were guided to the bridge. A gray-haired man in the dark-blue uniform of an officer was waiting for them.

"Lieutenant Desmond."

"General Linwei."

"Are you here to take over the ship?"

"Yes. From here on out, the *Witch Hunter* belongs to the Red Wind."

"What if I don't accept it?"

"I think you should consider my proposal carefully."

"What are you going to do? Take me prisoner? You'd rather be a pirate, huh, Desmond? Like in the old stories. Have you prepared a shark to throw us at?"

"There are no sharks, but I have prepared something more dangerous than sharks. Eternal darkness."

General Linwei kept his mouth shut.

Desmond said with a calm expression, " We've already taken over your commander's base. We've also taken control of the command post, and there's plenty of time to deal with you and your crew. Will you hand over control to us and join us, or will you become prisoners, or will you all die here?"

Linwei sighed. The crew on the bridge looked at him anxiously. Linwei knew that his luck had ended here. *This is the moment when the long chain of fate breaks.*

"I'm going to ask you one thing. Who moved the Red Wind?"

"We have a lot of friends. You know them well."

"I understand. I did too."

Linwei leaned against one horizontal part of the bridge's star map. On the map, the three planetary systems of the Planetary Union were projected in scale models. He wished he could've made one final voyage in this ship.

"Pass the boat, General," ordered Desmond.

"Desmond," said Linwei.

"Yes?"

"Fall to hell. You damn pirate."

Desmond gave a blank expression for a moment. Then he made a grim face and shot the general. The old man spewed blood as he flew backward and crashed into the corner of the bridge. Screams erupted from everywhere.

Desmond looked toward the ceiling and spoke calmly.

"That's why I hate condescending generals."

"We've taken control of the *Witch Hunter* and all the other ships. The other brothers seem to have succeeded as well."

"Okay, take off," Karan told Desmond through the comm link. "I'll be there soon."

"Yes, boss. I will prepare for takeoff."

Karan turned to the crew. "Move."

"What about the prisoners?" asked Theresia.

"We don't have time to take them with us. Soon the Valhalla Ground Forces and the off-planet squadron will notice something is wrong with the base. They may have already noticed."

Hearing this, the bound command room personnel clamored. Karan didn't care.

"Okay," said Theresia. "I think you should get out of here fast."

Karan nodded and ordered the brothers to move.

Theresia boarded the heavy cruiser *Canberra*, while Karan went to the *Witch Hunter*. As soon as Karan was on board,

Desmond told the pirate crew to prepare for take-off.

Half of the ship's manpower refused to cooperate and became prisoners of war, and half agreed to help the Red Wind pirates maneuver the ship. They ignited the engine and soon the gas began to rise. The other four ships did the same.

A large cruiser, two heavy cruisers, and two assault ships soon flew into the air.

Karan appeared on the bridge.

"Boss." Desmond nodded to him.

"Good job, Desmond. Open a communication channel to Gajin."

Once he'd done so, Karan said, "Gajin, wipe out the base with orbital bombardment."

"Copy that, Captain."

A long merchant ship floated above the base. It was a pirate bomber. Gajin activated the bombing system. The hull shook for a moment, and the explosives window opened.

Judy, who was sitting in the seat next to him, said, "I can't wait."

"Yeah. Hold on tight, there will be a kickback."

Judy grabbed his seat handle with a look of anticipation. "I'm ready. Hurry up."

Explosives began to fall to the ground from the explosives window at the bottom of the aircraft.

"They're off."

Elliptical-shaped objects appeared in the air—small tactical nuclear warheads. The warheads dropped toward the ground with a whistling sound.

The Valhalla Mobile Group base was destroyed. The flames raged like fireworks, eating the buildings to dust.

Karan whistled his approval. "What a beautiful sight."

Desmond looked down at the base where he had worked for years, as it was consumed by the explosive fire. He didn't know why he suddenly felt sentimental about its loss. He thought of Linwei, who had been shouting at him to go to hell. *Damn old man.*

Gajin communicated with the *Witch Hunter*. "Captain, there's something on the radar. It's in the outer orbit of Valhalla. It looks like an Allied fleet."

Karan got up from his seat. "They showed up sooner than I thought," he murmured. Louder, he said, "All ships, prepare for battle."

"Captain, we are the only ones here so far." Theresia's voice came through from the heavy cruiser *Canberra*.

"Hold on a little bit. The brothers are coming soon."

Arenaline rushed through every corner of Karan's body. His time had come for victory against the Alliance.

9.

On the morning after Jinsoo's visit, Danny saw someone put a plate of rice noodles and a few pieces of boiled pork under his cage. Danny focused on filling his stomach quickly rather than thinking more about the plate and the origins of the food. It would take a day or so for Aiden to notice that he was gone. Even then, Danny was beginning to worry his friend wouldn't have any way of tracking him down here in the Ganesh government's detention facilities.

Jinsoo, who appeared again the next day, confirmed the question.

"Danny, if you're hoping for a rescue, you're fooling yourself. Even if someone knows you're gone, they have no idea you're here. I hope you're seriously considering my proposal. Your assistance would be most helpful."

"Why don't you tell the commander yourself what you want?"

"We both know your grandfather wouldn't listen to me. But he might listen to you."

"Honestly, I don't want to convey your proposal to him, but I'm curious about the content. What do you want to negotiate about?"

Jinsoo smiled brightly. "Ultimately, we want to thoroughly guarantee the independent status of all planets. But for now, I think it will be fine if we separate the world we live in and the Alliance agrees to stay out of it."

"At the end of the day, how is what are you talking about any different from the collapse of the Union government system? Do you think I'm going to turn to your side?"

"I don't want you to turn right away. And I'm not advocating for a reset of all interplanetary relationships and interactions, as you may think. I just want you to understand us."

He brought a chair and sat a little closer to Danny with the iron bars in between them.

"Mr. Carlos, are you interested in the origins of the human race?"

"Why would I be interested in that? I know where we came from."

"Yes, yes. But what you know is just a fact. You, like most people, are ignorant of the full picture. I'm talking about how the migration project was conceived 600 years ago when four migrant fleets left Earth."

A little interest stirred in Danny. "Go on."

Jinsoo smiled contentedly. "Okay. Let's begin the story. The migrant fleet was planned ahead of the birth of a huge coalition government representing Earth and the solar system. It was a political body similar to the Planetary Union. The government of Korea, a small regional country, designed the *Hwanung*, which became the birthplace of the now-defunct government of the Mining Guild and its residents."

He paused for a moment. "The Korean culture followed the same naming convention as my original name. Geographically, it was a small country in the eastern part of the Asian continent. '*Hwanung*' means the god of heaven, the father of the first ancestors in their founding mythology. While building the ship, they must have thought that it would be the hero of the new space age. You haven't heard these stories before because access is completely blocked by the Union government. They are wary of anyone having a different identity.

"Anyway, around that time, in the year 2,280, barriers between small countries on Earth gradually disappeared, and social and linguistic boundaries and restrictions became blurred. The idea of a United Nations government was ripe. In most people's eyes, it would have been a sign of great unity. A monumental unification that was like a miracle of the century ahead of mankind, who had been at war with one another for too long. Danny, what do you think of the term 'grand unity'?"

Danny answered without hesitation, "It's not possible."

Jinsoo looked at him quietly, as if waiting for an explanation. When Danny said nothing else, Jinsoo continued, "A lot of things happened before the Desirée system was unified. If you count only the most recent 100 years, there was a First Name War and a Second Name War, and twenty years ago, there was the Big Crush on my home planet Han."

"Yeah, the Big Crush was horrible. But strictly speaking, it was an accident. Damn it, it was a one-sided attack by aliens with a higher civilization than us," said Danny, getting frustrated.

"Danny, it wasn't just an accident, like an asteroid crash. It involved the Planetary Union government."

Danny's expression darkened. "Are you going to start the bullshit you usually talk about?"

"You'll see for yourself whether I'm telling the truth or not. Or ask your grandfather."

Danny was silent for a moment. A moment later, a shrill voice escaped his mouth. "What do you mean?"

Jinsoo pretended not to hear and continued, "Anyway, back to the story. Like the Planetary Union government, Earth was on the verge of the Unified Earth Government—"

"Wait, what do you mean by what you just said? What does my grandfather have to do with anything?"

"As I said, the Union government was involved in the Big Crush. And your grandfather, Harry Carlos, is a commander of the Allied Defense Forces. He can probably tell you a lot of things. It's best if you hear them directly from him, Danny Carlos."

"You mean my grandfather was directly involved in the Big Crush? Is that what you're saying?"

Jinsoo shrugged his shoulders. "It could be."

"Tell me for sure!"

"Danny, do you want to hear something certain? What is certain is that tens of millions of people died that day, and the man in front of you is a dangerous person who is dreaming of revenge against those who destroyed his home planet. Is there anything more certain than this? The government put planet Han into the Union under the guise of protecting it. I'm sure your grandfather knows more about this, but I'm not going to tell you everything here. I don't know if I'm ready, and I'm worried how you'll react if

I tell you all the facts. So, you'd better keep pace with our conversation, so you can keep listening to me, okay?"

Several thoughts came to Danny. He had too many questions he wanted to ask, especially of his grandfather. But he nodded. "Okay."

"Okay. Let's continue the story. Of course, there were people like us among the people on the verge of great unification. They wondered, 'Is great unification possible?' 'If there really is a great unification, what good will it bring to us?' It makes sense, because the inauguration of a unified humanitarian government does not mean that the same level of welfare and benefits will be provided to all members of small cultures. Humans are selfish creatures. People are willing to help if their family or friends are in pain, but they are stingy when it comes to strangers suffering from starvation on a distant continent. So, not all problems facing humanity would be solved at once.

"The leaders and people of various small countries in the mother district also thought the plan for unity would not come to fruition in the way they desired. So, they planned an expedition to outer space to build their own unity. Planetary sites where they could leave their seeds. It was a plan to secure the land to which they would migrate, no matter what their unertain future might bring, when a unified human government on Earth would one day be established. Of course, it wasn't limited to those countries. It was an expensive adventure at the time to build such a migrant ship and sail to distant stars at speeds close to the speed of light. So, they got project sponsorship from other small countries as well. This is why 50 to 60 percent of the world's human race is descended from the residents of three East Asian countries and Australia, while the rest are descendants from all human countries.

"Our ancestors wanted to establish independent and peaceful republics and maintain friendship with one another. Mr. Carlos, this is why the Union government shouldn't exist. The present Planetary Union is not the world our ancestors wanted. Do you think the Union government and Amon Soros provides equal treatment and welfare to all planetary members? Do you think it doesn't discriminate against the inhabitants of all planets? You are a Carlos, and your father and grandfather were Carlos, because your grandfather bought the right to inherit the name. But what about the rest who didn't? Their treatment is lower than that of a dog. How about my compatriots on planet Han? The people of Valhalla, who were recently joined to the Union, are not allowed to have surnames, right? Is this the great unity you want?"

Danny had to clear his mind for a moment before answering. "All these stories sound plausible, but I'm not convinced yet."

"Go on," said Jinsoo.

"For what you just said to be persuasive," continued Danny, "it must be supported by evidence from actual events. One is, 'Was the Union government really involved in the Big Crush?' And the other is, 'Is Valhalla really being treated unfairly?' I honestly think the Valhalla thing is harsh. I have a feeling most of the Union's residents would agree, even if they don't say so openly. But as you know, it was the Valhalans who attacked Allied forces first. This is a problem that time will solve. Problems that arise between the occupying forces and the occupiers will eventually end in the right direction. And when it comes to the Big Crush, you still haven't told me the whole story. You have to provide solid evidence for the case."

Jinsoo's mouth formed a gloomy smile. "Do you know why I told you this, Danny? Because you were very close to your uncle Yeonsu Carlos. As you may know, my friend Karl and your uncle stole the *Admiral Cheng Ho* and headed to the Earth we longed for. Like your uncle, I thought you would understand us."

"You're mistaken. I haven't seen or talked to him since the day he disappeared. So, I don't understand what he was thinking."

"You'll understand us too. Danny, I want to confirm something with you."

"What?"

Jinsoo got up from his seat and pressed the button on the device he was holding in his hand.

A mechanical sound echoed in the room, and the grate of Danny's cage went up. The electric curtain that had seen a slight flow out of the grate seemed to have disappeared.

Danny eyed Jinsoo warily. "Are you going to let me go?"

"No. I have something I want to show you and ask you. I'm keeping an eye on you from an unseen place to see if you'll unlock your telekinetic powers, so don't think about trying anything foolish. Follow me, Danny."

Danny left the room and saw similar cage rooms lined the hallway. Jinsoo was already way ahead. He hurried to keep up with him. Soon he noticed that Ari and the bulky man had appeared from behind him.

"How are you?" said Danny warmly.

Ari glanced at him. "Never been better, Carlos."

"Thanks for a good rest for a few days."

Ari raised an eyebrow. "You're very welcome."

"Can you get me out of here now?"

The young woman shook her head with an elegant gesture. "Ask Jinsoo about that."

"I thought we got along well."

"I wouldn't count on it."

The emotionless look Ari gave Danny made him shut his mouth. Flirting was not going to get him anywhere with this woman.

After turning on the light through his handy tool, Jinsoo led them down one more floor. They entered a large, dark hall. In the corner was another square room about five meters wide and five meters long. Danny couldn't see much around the hall, but he thought this place might be a concentration camp, or some kind of lab, or both.

"This was originally an early biology laboratory," said Jinsoo, as if he could read Danny's thoughts. "It was a place where settlers who moved to Ganesh studied the creatures they found while terraforming it. They initially thought there wouldn't be any advanced life here, due to the poisonous sulfur gas that the land harbors. It was a surprising discovery for them when they found there were giant animals that lived on sulfuric acid.

"The animals reacted very lethally to oxygen. Biologists who came to Ganesh confined the animals and conducted various experiments to study the ecology of Ganesh. They are all extinct now, but they were creatures that were created in a different world from humans. Since then, this lab has been mainly used as a Union political prison camp. Until we took it over, that is."

"What do you have locked up here?"

Jinsoo Kim made a sad expression, peering at the shadows waving in the dark. "It's my colleague."

He turned on the power to the laboratory, and a glow-ing white light filled the hall.

Danny frowned. A man was locked up in a glass labora-tory room ahead of them.

The man had twisted limbs. His torso was twisted at a bizarre angle under his head. The man looked at them through the wide laboratory window and opened his mouth.

A non-human scream erupted.

Danny covered his ears with his hands. "What is that?"

The man slammed his head into the thick glass window. His eyelids were crushed, and blood spattered.

Danny said in disbelief, "Who is this guy? What the hell is he doing?"

"That's exactly what I wanted to ask you," said Jinsoo.

"What?"

"This man is our colleague Hogan. He was sent to the sea planet Neptunus, a satellite of New Sydney. He was sent to spy on the Union water facility and infiltrate a secret facility there, and then came back like this. What the hell is my colleague? I thought you would know."

Danny shook his head. "I don't even understand what's going on, let alone how this happened."

Danny saw something sprout from the man's arm.

"That…" said Danny helplessly.

"Yeah. It's an arm."

On the forearm and biceps of the man's arm sprouted small, slender, fern-like arms. They reminded Danny of the arms of a baby, as they shook and trembled. Turning away, Danny began to vomit.

Jinsoo spoke in a bitter tone. "What the hell did the Allies do to my comrades, Danny?"

The man slammed his head against the window again. Brain water splashed against the glass.

IO.

On the morning three days after Hypkeranos informed Joshua that the hearing was going on, a messenger from the Diutin Council came to him with Hyp. The messenger was an alien with a slightly larger stature than Hypkeranos, golden hair, and scars resembling razors on his arms. He wore gold ornaments. He introduced himself as Aureus.

"You mean this afternoon?" asked Joshua.

Aureus, equipped with an interpreter, spoke fluently in the official language of the Desirée system. "Yes, human. Victoranus, a member of the council, and I will come here directly after we are ready."

"Call me Joshua. Why don't you call me to the council room?"

"This is the first time that a human has visited our world. At least as far as I know. Research and response to the bacteria from the outside world you carry with you are still ongoing. We must prepare just in case something might happen. For that reason, the council made the decision that the hearing in this special case can be carried out in an abbreviated fashion here. The hearing committee entrusts all the decisions to me and the members of the legislature."

"Okay. What time should I expect you here? It seems that you, the Diutin people, live twice as long as us, so your notion of time is a bit relaxed compared to ours. One year here is roughly two years on our world," said Joshua. He was quite impatient to get this over with.

"The hearing will be over in one day. Senator Victoranus and I will be conducting the proceedings together, and we don't like to waste time. We will briefly review the facts and proceed with an overview of the case."

"Hyp, are you coming too?"

Hypkeranos shook his head. "No."

Joshua nodded. "Okay. After the hearing, when will the trial be held?"

Hipp answered, "It will begin in a few days."

The aliens said goodbye to Joshua and left the room. Joshua let out a long sigh of frustration.

When the Diutinians returned to the Visitor's Tower that afternoon, Joshua was with Cassie. A message popped up on the screen in Cassie's room requesting that Joshua go to the small meeting room on the twentieth floor. As he got up from his chair, Cassie hugged him.

"Come back safely."

Joshua kissed her, then went out and climbed into the elevator at the end of the corridor. The elevator reached the twentieth floor in seconds. When he got off, the warrior Dayweo stood waiting for him.

"Dayweo?"

"My role is to guide you. Just follow me."

Joshua did so. After walking for about three minutes, Dayweo stopped in front of a door with several screens attached to it. He reached out to the screen, and a biometric scan began. After a moment, the door disappeared. Dayweo pointed inward.

As Joshua entered the conference room, he saw Aureus and an alien he had never seen before sitting next to him.

"Sit here," said the new alien.

Joshua sat down on the metal chair he was pointing to. Even though it was metal, it had a soft texture.

"Nice to meet you, Joshua Kwon. I am Victoranus. I am a member of the council, and I am also the commander of the Adola Defense Force. I went to your home planet, Han, ten years ago, about twenty years ago in human time."

Sparks flew from Joshua's eyes. "Are you the one who bombed the planet Han and slaughtered my people?"

Victoranus didn't change his expression. Rather, Aureus, who was sitting next to him, reacted to Joshua's words by twitching. Joshua had gotten used to Diutinians' expressions through Hyp, but he could not read Victoranus's face. *Is this a Diutin-style poker face?*

"There are a lot of stories out there, Joshua Kwon. But this hearing has nothing to do with that case. So, let's get back to the point. I'm just trying to confirm a few basic facts, so please answer them as honestly as possible. First of all, are you Joshua Kwon, the captain of the ship claiming to be *Robespierre*?"

"Yes."

"How did you get to know Hypkeranos?"

Joshua thought of the day he'd lost everything. "On the day you brought a warship and ravaged the planet Han, I lost my wife and daughter. Since then, I have been wandering among the countless corpses. Her name was Amy, though I doubt you care about that."

Victoranus was speechless.

Joshua continued, "Do you know how the survivors were supposed to live? The government collapsed, and there were corpses everywhere. Desolation and corpses and hunger were all we had. Supplies from the Union government arrived two weeks later. At that time, planet Han's Mining Guild government was not a member of the Union of humans, so that's why it was so hot. They also controlled the sending of supplies from Amaterasu, the nearest planet to Han. Amaterasu was a member of the Union government, so they had to follow instructions. Anyway, for two weeks we did everything we could to survive. We ate the corpses. The taste was so deadly. To tell you the truth, though, I've never had such delicious meat in my life."

Victoranus raised his hand. "Take care of yourself and only talk about what you need to, human."

"First of all, if you want to know how I met Hypkeranos, you must listen to all these stories, Senator. Then you will understand better. I don't know if you're ready to hear my story."

"We are ready," Aureus said.

Joshua continued the tale. "I was a space force pilot on Han. My rank was lieutenant. I gathered my surviving men and their families and set up a camp at the Space Force Base. Together with the men, I packed up the scarce supplies and defended my men and my people by defeating the robbers of the villagers. The Planetary Union government sent supplies, but those supplies were not enough. And that's all the government did—oh, except for incorporate us into the Union government. During that time, my hometown was in anarchy. One day while watching the universe at that base camp, I found out that your ship was moored over the planet, watching us."

Joshua laughed until his mouth ripped open. "What do you think I did?"

"Did you attack?" said Victoranus.

Joshua nodded. "That's right. I regrouped the few remaining squadrons and attacked your ship. We were so easily subdued. The crew rendered me and my companions' fighters useless, and soon we were captured inside the huge ship. The ship's commander was Hypkeranos."

Joshua thought back to when he first met Hyp. He remembered the fear pounding in his heart as he and his colleagues were guided to the bridge. He was expecting to die. He was ready for it. He wanted to go be with his wife and daughter.

But Hyp hadn't killed him. Instead, Hypkeranos had led them to his office and introduced himself as the Vice-Captain of the Adola System Defense Corps. He then told Joshua that he thought humanity was an aggressor.

Victoranus said in a meaningful voice, "That action can be seen as very aggressive in some cases, especially for a race that has been at war for a long time like us. Anyway, we were very upset when three of your ships appeared in the Adola system. Using warp-drive technology in that way. We were the first civilization to create a drive. In conclusion, you have violated the Diutin Federation's sailing protocol. Even the few intelligent civilizations that interact with us exchange a list in advance of ships with warp-speed capabilities, as is required under the Warp Convention. It's unfortunate."

"And one of those three ships declared war on you, so you counted them as enemies?"

"Yes. We had no reason not to believe you were an aggressor. That's why we defined you as enemies and followed you as you fled to your motherland. To prevent further retaliation in the future."

"Wrong. You are slayers. Hypkeranos knew that and was watching us without returning to Adola."

Victoranus sighed. It was his first emotional reaction.

Aureus, who had been silent for a while, spoke. "Then he reported that he would monitor the dynamics of human civilization. Did he offer you our technology as an apology, Joshua?"

"He apologized to me. He was only telling the truth. He told me that one of the three ships from our system had declared war on you. There are records of your people appearing several times in Desirée over hundreds of years with minerals. There are certainly some interpreters among us who understand your language, but they have never appeared on one of your planets. Those three ships were clearly sent by the Allied government."

Joshua's expression contorted. "I knew then. My home planet had fallen into the trap of the Union government. The one who declared war on you must have been an interpreter ship sent by the Union to the Mining Guild government. Hypkeranos told me that, and I informed him that the ships were dispatched not for aggression, but for goodwill. Senator Victoranus, sixty million people evaporated that day. Isn't it very sad that it was caused by a misunderstanding?"

"So, Hypkeranos was …"

"Hypkeranos was astonished by the actions of the Planetary Union government, which had plunged their people into such a quagmire. I said on the spot that I would not forgive them. I will attack them until the day I die, and I will die to see the Union government collapse. Then Hypkeranos gave me the ship he was on, the ship we later named *Robespierre*."

Victoranus and Aureus looked at each other.

Aureus asked, "Is that statement true?"

"Yes. That's how we became friends. And the Union nightmare, Discarded, was born."

Jinsoo cut off the power to the laboratory. Before it went out, Danny made eye contact with Hogan in the laboratory.

Darkness descended.

Hogan was silent.

Jinsoo said, "Everyone, let's go up."

They went back up to a higher level. It was the floor of the room where Danny had been detained. He was getting tired of the dark.

Jinsoo led him to another room. Ari and the hulking man disappeared, leaving Jinsoo and Danny behind. Before they left, Jinsoo thanked them. Danny sat down. The room was decorated in neat sepia tones, and teacups and teaware were displayed in a cupboard. Jinsoo took out a white porcelain cup, boiled coffee beans, and made coffee. A faint scent soon spread throughout the room. Jinsoo put milk in one cup of coffee.

"You?"

Danny shook his head. Jinsoo nodded and poured a second cup of coffee. Danny was feeling a bit better after vomiting. He sipped his coffee and said, "Did you say that man was sent to Neptunus?"

"That's right. I hoped you would know something about what happened to him, Carlos."

"I'm sorry, but I've never seen anything like that before. It's like something out of a horror movie."

"It's disappointing. Anyway, I'm sure your allies did this. My men were sent to a secret facility and then escaped. Yukyung, who brought Hogan here, is still undergoing psychiatric treatment. She lost her fiancé there. I heard about it. I don't know if he was sane, but the corpses of the dead crew that appeared before takeoff ate up her fiancé. Seeing how Hogan was when they arrived, I couldn't even dismiss her story as just bullshit."

Jinsoo took a sip of his coffee.

"Danny, I'm going to let you go."

Danny looked at the man opposite him with suspicious eyes. "Really?"

"Really."

"Why?"

"I don't think we're going to gain anything more by keeping you here. And you can't stop us anyway. Besides, you are Carlos's dear nephew."

"I don't understand. Thank you for letting me go, but you'll regret it. Wouldn't it be better to reduce the Allied force's power even a little? Did you forget that I was one of the few Allied soldiers with telekinetic abilities?"

"Then I should kill you right here?"

Danny shut his mouth. He looked at Jinsoo's movement. If Danny opened up his abilities, Jinsoo could respond at any time.

Jinsoo laughed. "You don't want that, and neither do I. Anyway, I'm just as talented as you are, and seeing people with abilities somehow gives me a sense of camaraderie. You must have had a hard life like me. Danny, like your uncle, I hope you will come to understand what my people are fighting for… And I hope to see you again."

Danny pondered what to say. But no matter how much he thought about it, he didn't want to salute the separatists. Even in spite of the truth Jinsoo had told him and the appearance of Hogan.

"I don't know if I'll see you again, but I hope you'll change your mind, too," said Danny. "If you haven't started, you'd better reconsider. This is reckless."

"Oh, no. The war is already underway. The attack has begun in Valhalla and the Allied task force has been anni-hilated. It has also begun here in Ganesh. I must go join them soon."

Danny's eyes widened. "What?"

"A lot has happened in the days you've been here."

Jinsoo got up from his seat and pointed to a door on the other side of the room. Light was leaking out of it.

"After you finish your coffee, open the door over there, Danny. Then you'll see the land you've been longing to see."

Jinsoo opened the drawer under his seat, took out an item, and handed it to him. It was Danny's handy tool. Danny took it and pushed his left hand into it.

"See you again, Carlos," said Jinsoo.

Danny pondered his words that the war had already begun. He downed the last of his coffee and got up.

The light leaking from the door was calling out to Danny.

Three hours had passed since the hearing ended. Joshua was pacing in his room, waiting to hear the results. Cassie was watching him silently. Joshua spoke, suddenly remembered something.

"Cassie. How did it go with Yuna?"

"We had fun. We spent some time in the garden again."

"Oh, that's good."

He looked like he didn't even understand what was good. Cassie crossed his arms, slightly annoyed at him.

"Joshua, can you stop pacing and just sit down? This restlessness isn't helping anything."

"I'm sorry, Cassie." He sighed and sat down.

"Do you want some coffee?" She brought some over to him.

He looked delighted. "Where did you get it?" he asked.

"Drink. I worked very hard to find what was left. Mei gave it to me."

"Mei? Jeez, how's she doing?"

"Even if you're too preoccupied, I'm checking the status of our colleagues who were brought here once in a while, so don't worry. They understand what you're going through."

After the hearing, Victoranus had said that the results would be decided within a few hours. Joshua knew the Diutins would eventually bring him to court. But it mattered what the charges were. Hypkeranos said it was a felony to use wormhole navigation techniques by a different race. However, Joshua had made it clear to Victoranus and Aureus that he had no choice but to do so, after misunderstandings had led to the Diutinians slaughtering mankind.

What charges would he face in court? Joshua felt a little bit of peace as the coffee circulated throughout his body.

Someone knocked on the door. Joshua jumped up.

Cassie approached, grabbed the doorknob, and looked at Joshua for a moment. He nodded.

The door opened and Hypkeranos entered. Hypkeranos looked perplexed. From that look on his face, Joshua's anticipation vanished.

He asked in a calm voice, "Did the results come out?"

Hypkeranos nodded. "The first trial will be held in three days, in the form of a council trial."

"Any charges?"

"As expected. Unauthorized technology use and leaks. It will be a felony."

Joshua felt his strength drain.

"That's ridiculous!" There was anger in Cassie's voice. "Didn't they hear Joshua's story? If leaking wormhole technology is a felony, you mean that the genocide committed by the Diutin before that wasn't taken into account, right?"

Hypkeranos's expression darkened. "I don't know how the laws of our people differ from your laws, but we don't take into account details from separate cases. That should be dealt with separately."

"But—"

"It's okay, Cassie." Joshua stopped her. He spoke to Hypkeranos with a supremely calm expression. "Three days from now?"

"That's correct."

"Thank you for helping me so far, but can you help me a little more, Hyp? What can I do to prepare?"

Hypkeranos looked at Joshua for a moment without answering, then said, "You don't need to prepare."

"What?"

"You just have to answer truthfully to whatever questions they ask."

"Hyp, what are you talking about?"

Hypkeranos sat down on his chair, supporting his head

with one hand. "I'm the, not you. The charge of indictment is that I broke the precepts and intervened in the affairs of a different race, illegally remodeling a ship belonging to the Diutinians, and providing it with wormhole technology to a different race without permission. You're going to be a witness in this trial. They don't want to forgive me. They're going to bring me down to hell, Joshua."

II.

The first thing Danny was aware of when he stepped outside was sound. Shouts, cracks, buzzes, rattles, cracklings… There was a light in the middle of the noise. The blue sun, Shennong, burned. Danny put his hand to his forehead for a moment and then narrowed his eyes. The air was cold. While his eyes adapted quickly to the light, his body needed more time to adapt to the chilly air.

When Danny opened his eyes again, he saw a slope. He looked around for a moment at the recessed door toward the floor from which he came out and the nearby bush, before moving on. Where were these sounds coming from? Obviously, Jinsoo had told him that this facility was a Ganesh government facility. But Danny had no idea where he was.

He initialized his handy tool. Although the communication address book was deleted, communication could be received, but it was impossible to transmit a message to anyone unless the other party's signal address was memorized. He couldn't contact Aiden or anyone in the Alliance.

As he moved along the slope, he saw a familiar city sideways. It was evident that his present location was on the western outskirts of the city. Danny made his way down the slope and recognized that the river under the bridge ahead was the Lu River, which ran through the city. There was no one on the bridge. It was afternoon, but he didn't see anyone around. He carefully crossed the bridge.

The entrance to the road leading to the shops appeared. An Android G popped out and looked at Danny, holding out the latest version of a handy tool. "Do you need a handy tool? The handy tool of the Granot Group provides you with a variety of experiences. Entertainment, communication, medical care, space leaps, muscle strengthening, and near-death sexual experiences. What are you interested in?"

Danny thought for a moment. "Um, honestly, the last field is a little intriguing, but that's okay. I don't want to get distracted. My handy tool has been reset, though, and it's quite inconvenient. Is there anything wrong with the city right now, G? What the hell are these noises? Was there a riot in the city?"

Android G answered, "Militants have gathered in the heart of the city. The level of violence has gone beyond simple riots and is on the verge of engagement with the army. Several humans are also moving in groups on the periphery."

"Damn. What's the recommended route?"

"Most routes have a high probability of encountering numerous clashes and hostilities. The possibilities are too numerous to recommend. My best recommendation is to leave the city via the eastern skyway on the least likely route." The android paused for a moment. "The A-wings are parked there."

"Okay, thanks."

Danny took the path the android showed him.

After three blocks, Danny saw a woman screaming by the road in an alleyway. A man hit her in the face, and the woman fainted. Danny paused for a moment. Five or six young men with guns dragged the woman away. One of them looked at Danny and grinned. A laser flew from somewhere and burned the alleyway the group had just disappeared down.

Danny struggled to erase the woman from his memory, and moved on, taking advantage of the chaos. Robbers and rioters were fighting in every direction.

Danny's handy tool rang.

"Danny? Where the hell are you?"

"Aiden? I'm on Dead Dogs Street."

"It's crazy, Danny. I'm not kidding. Your bio-signs didn't show up, so I kept looking."

"Right, damn. Can you come here?"

"They have anti-aircraft guns. I might be shot down on the way. I'll send you a rendezvous point, so get there as fast as you can, and I'll meet you. It's dangerous to be running around alone. Are you armed?"

"No, I'm not."

"Please try to avoid fighting as much as possible."

"Yeah, I'm not that stupid."

Aiden's communication ended. Danny looked at the coordinates displayed on the handy tool. He changed course. If there were dangerous guys walking around with anti-aircraft guns, it was impossible to know if they could avoid being shot down even if they rode the ownerless

A-wing. He noticed that the rendezvous point was a hilly southern hill, about a thirty-minute walk from his location.

As Danny moved south, he saw all kinds of commotion in the streets. The civilians were being subdued by soldiers. They didn't look like Root Restorationists. Their weapons were poor, and they didn't appear to be driven by any command. Danny glanced at the wreckage of the collapsed building, then telekinetically cleared the wreckage and moved on.

About ten minutes later, when the road narrowed south, someone spoke behind Danny.

"Who are you?"

Danny spun around to see soldiers in Allied battle uniforms with plasma rifles. He let out a relieved breath.

"Captain Danny Carlos."

"Allied forces?"

The man who appeared to be the commander murmured while looking at his handy tool and Danny alternately.

"Danny Carlos…Captain. A member of the Third Regiment of the Second Star System Defense Force… Third Regiment? Are you a member of the Hound Dog Squadron?"

"That's right."

"And you are a talented person, a valuable resource for the Allied forces. I am Sergeant Haman of the Third Reconnaissance Division of the Eighth Corps, and these are my platoon members."

"What are the stats on the enemies?"

"There are tens of thousands of men. They're even properly armed. The central part of the city is in chaos. But they'll be put down soon. Where have you been, Captain?"

"I was detained by Jinsoo Kim."

Sergeat Harman's eyes widened.

"Kim Jinsoo…? The head of the Root Restorationists? You met him?"

"Yes, I was beaten by him. I didn't think he would be as talented as me. I was vigilant."

"You must have suffered a lot. Anyway, I'm glad I've met you. I'll help you get back to the Defense Command. Come with us."

"Thank you, Sergeant, but it's okay. I was on my way to the rendezvous point with the help of my crew."

"Oh, you don't have to decline. We'll take you there. Let's get going," he said to the other soldiers

Danny thought the sergeant was stubborn. A sergeant's shoulder strap pattern came into his view as he was thinking for a moment. It was a pattern with two fish facing left and right. Danny's body stiffened.

"Sergeant Harman."

Sergeant Haman turned and looked at him. "Yes, Captain?"

"Did you say the Eighth Corps Reconnaissance Team?"

"Yes?"

Sergeant Haman made a puzzled expression.

"Which star are you chasing? A star or none?" asked Danny.

It was a famous greeting. Seventy years ago, during the First Name War, in a time of extreme chaos when it was impossible to distinguish who was an ally, the Allied forces would ask unidentified people to say hello. This greeting was often used among the citizens at the time on the planet Ganesh, where there were more war victims than New Shanghai.

Sergeant Harman's face contorted. "I am not chasing

any stars."

Harman and his crew raised their plasma rifles and aimed at Danny.

"That's right, Captain. The star we're after isn't New Shanghai. You're a smart one, huh?"

"That fish pattern. It's the Ganesh government army's pattern. And there's no way the Allied forces are patrolling the city center leisurely. They're probably catching all your spies as we speak."

Haman nodded briefly. "You saw it right."

All over the planet Ganesh, the Root Resotrationists and the Ganesh garrison corps would be fighting against the Allied forces. And the Allied forces were surely having a hard time fighting on the ground. It would be difficult to tell who was an ally and who was an enemy with the naked eye. Danny tensed, waiting to see what Haman might do to him. But of course, givens Danny's powers, Sergeant Harman couldn't predict the outcome of the engagement. Danny didn't want to bleed unnecessarily.

The sound of an aircraft moving was heard in the distance. Haman raised his hand.

"Stop aiming. Return," he ordered his troops. "Go, Captain. I won't stop you. Not walking around here will prolong your life even a little."

Haman and his men disappeared. Danny relaxed.

As the wind blew, an assault ship appeared in the air. It was the flagship of the Third Regiment, *Little Boy*.

Once the flagship landed, Danny hurried on board. Aiden greeted him.

"Why are you late, Danny?"

"I ran into some enemies. It was the Ganesh government army, but I only found out later that they were traitors."

"What? How'd you escape them without a scratch?"

"They just let me go. I noticed a ship was coming. They were trying to avoid unnecessary sacrifices." Danny paused for a moment, then said, "And they may have thought that the situation would not change much if they let me go. How is Ganesh now, Aiden?"

Aiden shrugged with gloomy eyes. "I'll show you as we go. This way. The crew is waiting for you."

Danny grinned at the sight of his colleagues. It had been over a month since he'd seen them last. One-eyed sharpshooter Kirox trembled at him, asking if he was alive. Lu Xun, who was small in stature, but was the best in handling rifles and managing the organs, gripped Danny's shoulder and smiled.

"Is that enough of a greeting for you, Captain?" asked Aiden.

"Captain? Who, me?"

"Danny, you are the new captain of the *Little Boy*."

"What?"

"The order was issued immediately after you disappeared. You became the captain of the *Little Boy* in place of our missing training captain."

Lu Xun chuckled. Danny thought about Yeonsu Carlos for a moment. He swallowed hard.

Aiden said, " Captain, I think we will have to leave Ganesh exclusively for the agency. We will set the route to New Shanghai. Please give us the final order."

Danny said, "Okay, Aiden. Full speed to the engine. As soon as we leave the atmosphere, let's proceed with a sub-light speed drive at full speed."

"We will proceed at 40 percent of the speed of light."

"Perfect."

The ship flew through the red atmosphere with a shield up to keep it hidden from view. Danny saw the scene unfolding on the ground through a magnified screen. All kinds of armored vehicles and armored robots were broken and bodies were lined up. A lot of them looked like Allied forces.

"On the ground they've definitely won," said Aiden grimly.

Small battlebots half the size of Allied robots, armed with conventional pulse cannons, were hunting the Allies while walking on the ground on four legs.

"In space, engaged with Discarded and the Ganesh government Allied fleet."

As the atmosphere faded, the dark space where light disappeared gradually widened. It was outer space beyond the planet Ganesh. Thousands of battle squadrons, cruisers, and raiders rushed and fired their artillery.

Danny could see that there was still a stalemate in the space war. The Allied forces' fleet power was functioning properly.

"We weren't asked to join in the fighting?"

Kirox objected. "Danny—er, Captain, sorry. We are not well armed and we have not received any formal orders. The order we received is to take the captain and return to New Shanghai."

"Did my grandfather give the order, Kirox?"

"That's right, Commander Carlos's command. Let's go back first, Captain."

Danny thought of what Jinsoo Kim had said about his grandfather. "Okay, let's go back, guys."

He had stories to ask Harry Carlos.

The *Little Boy* entered sub-light flight mode. It took three hours to get to New Shanghai.

12.

The *Moscow* was engaged in the Battle of Ganesh, and shot down an Allied squadron from the top row. The assault ships of the Ganesh government forces charged the enemy cruisers, while Discarded's giants supported them with volleys.

The captain, Yuri, was watching from the bridge of the ship. Kamura's communication played over the loudspeaker.

"Captain, their defenses are strong. They're doing a lot of damage, and we've lost a lot of ships."

Yuri nodded, focused. "Okay, Kamura. Haneul, get us connected with Kim Jinsoo."

"Aye, Captain," said Haneul Bravo.

After a while, Jinsoo appeared at the bottom of the screen.

"Dear Captain Yuri."

"Jinsoo. Currently, the war situation here is deadlocked. Is the ground cleared up?"

"The Allied ground forces were almost wiped out. The

fleet seems to be struggling quite a bit. It's a pity that *Robespierre* would have been a lot of help right about now."

"Don't even think that's something you can hope for right now. Do you have any troops to send?"

"Are you at a disadvantage?"

"The less sacrifices the better."

"Okay. We'll finish the cleanup soon and send the armored robots there. They're the ones who can help with air warfare."

"Thank you."

"By the way, I met Danny Carlos."

"What?" blurted Yuri. She couldn't keep the shock from her voice.

Jinsoo was silent for a moment. "Do you know him?"

Yuri swallowed hard, collecting herself. "I knew him when I was a spy in Altra, the capital of New Shanghai."

"I thought you might have known him. I figured I'd tell you first."

"It's okay, Jinsoo. How did you come to meet him?"

"This time, he was working as a spy in Ganesh. He was noticed by my comrades. I didn't know at first that he was Harry Carlos's grandson. We talked about a lot of things, and I tried to convince him to join us. He hasn't completely turned around, but I have a feeling he might find out the truth later and stand on our side."

"What did you talk about?"

"I told him a little bit about the Big Crush and planet Han. We'll see, Yuri."

"Okay." She shook her head to re-focus on the task at hand. "Send me an armored robot for space use."

"Will do, Captain." Jinsoo disappeared.

Yuri's heart was pounding. *Danny, it's foul of you to*

suddenly reappear in my life like this.

She suspected this was some kind of prank. She'd left Danny. Even before the day of Discarded's attack on Altra, Yuri had been preparing to part with him—forever.

Haneul Bravo's voice brought her back to reality. "Captain, the squadron of this ship broke through the right side of the enemy's assault ship. If it continues like this, the squadron will soon be annihilated!"

Yuri's eyes lit up.

"Shall we call a backup squadron?" Haneul said with urgency.

If they left the squadron like this, soon the Allied forces would dig into the collapsed right side of the camp and it would be a melee battle in an instant. But it would take too long for reinforcements to arrive from the ground.

"No, I'm not calling."

Haneul pressed her lips together. Yuri knew she was thinking of her lover, Junkou Meg, who was out there in that fight.

"The assault of the land squadron smashed the enemy cruisers for the third time," another commander said. But in the air, everything was still a mess.

The moment had come when the war situation would be turned upside down if Yuri made the slightest mistake. Allied forces were attacking with all their might. If they could block this attack and counterattack, the combined fleet of Discardid and Ganesh could win.

But what if we can't stop this attack?

Yuri had to make a decision.

"Comrade Yuri Ivanova, things don't look very good." Karan Shetty's voice mixed with the cold mechanical sound.

"Karan?"

"Yeah, it's me. Why is it so hard to contact you? Do I have to come in person?"

"Oh my God, you always surprise me, Karan."

Karan burst into laughter. "The surprises aren't over yet, Yuri. See you in a little bit. First, clean up those ugly people."

Yuri saw the spaceships of the Red Wind Brotherhood appearing from afar on the right side of the screen, heading toward the Allied fleet.

13.

Karan looked at the war situation on the ship's star map. The Allied fleet had cruisers and destroyers attacking Yuri's fleet on both wings, starting from the form of five carriers with various combat squadrons placed in the middle of an invisible net. On the other hand, the Discarded and Ganesh had deployed destroyers and cruisers with strong firepower, centering on the *Moscow*. In addition, mine-laying ships were used to provoke the Allied assault ships to rush in. In the rear, the support ships were constantly moving, using nanotechnology to preserve the durability of the aircraft.

If one side was thoroughly focused on attacking, the other side was focused on defense and was looking for opportunities. Karan knew how this composition had come to be. Although the ships of the Ganesh government forces had joined in, it was difficult to withstand the immense firepower of the Allied forces.

Karan frowned. "Jena, Desmond, are you watching?"

A hologram of Jena and Desmond appeared on the right side of the star map.

Jena's hologram said. "I'm watching. I feel stuffy, as if my stomach is bloated."

"Me too. Ganesh nerds seem to be going to war, and they're gonna go ahead and attack them like this all day long. But this isn't my style. Desmond, what do you think?"

"I'd rather crush it and put my statue in its place."

Karan burst out laughing. "Can you? What are you going to do?"

"We plan to focus our photon cannon fire on the center, then charge right through them and cross them. But we'll need some support to do that."

"Are you going to counterattack after that?"

"The enemies on the other side of the cross section have to be dealt with by those crouching over there."

Karan nodded to the holograms with a satisfied expression. "Desmond, Jena, lead the fleet and attack the center together. Attack the rest of the ships as well. Theresia, you lead the brothers in the back row and attack their carrier with me."

"Captain, are you sure?" Jena said in disbelief.

"Trust Brother Desmond, Jena. Yuri, can you hear me? Our fleet is going to begin a two-way operation. I'll split them in two and I'll attack the carrier in the meantime. Let's do something useful together."

"We are few in number," Yuri replied over the ship's speaker. "Are you sure about this, Karan?"

"When have you ever had a numerical advantage? When the moment comes, don't spare your firepower."

"Okay. I'll trust you."

Yuri's communication sound disappeared. Karan's body

heated up as adrenaline pumped through his veins. *Let's do this.*

About twenty Brotherhood ships split into two groups and started maneuvering.

A mechanical sound echoed through the sharp air of the swampy land that dug into Jinsoo's nose.

From afar, an endless procession of residents surrounded the Ganesh government building and shouted. Jinsoo lifted his tired eyes and carved these scenes into his memory. He thought of a man who wasn't here. *Karl, we did it.*

The remains of the armored robots were scattered across the swamp. The corpses of the soldiers were starting to stink, even those that were only a day old.

"You look good," said a voice.

Jinsoo turned to look at the short man as he came into view.

"Governor."

Ganesh's head of government, Sakai Hashimoto, smiled awkwardly. Governor Sakai covered his nose as he looked at the decaying corpses.

"You've come a long way."

"How many corpses have you made, leader of the Root Restorationists?"

Jinsoo frowned slightly. "It's a great achievement, Governor. You don't seem to be very happy about it."

"Yes, it's a big achievement, but there's always a price, like the soldiers rotting over there."

"They are oppressors."

"And until recently, their leader was also my colleague."

Jinsoo looked at the governor's face for a moment. "You must be upset. I apologize for not seeing that."

"No need to apologize. My only concern is if we can control the factors that in any way hinder the success of this revolution. In other words, if we can recognize and carefully address those factors in advance, that will heighten our chances of success. I say this in the hope that the Discarded, the Roots, and other resistances will think of this."

"The governor is not happy with the consequences of the blood of his enemies."

"Blood calls for blood. The best solution was a diplomatic solution. It came to this point because it broke down. One thing I want to say to you is that it's better not to entice the enemy to hold too much of a grudge against us. And let go of the enemy factor. Could it also be a small stumbling block to the success of our revolution?" The governor smiled bitterly. "In Ganesh, there are a lot of equipment and personnel who will be my eyes and ears. Don't forget that the facility where you detained that man was lent by me, Jinsoo."

From the time he'd met the governor to plan a revolution, Jinsoo had thought he was unusual. Jinsoo admired him.

"I haven't forgotten. And I let Danny Carlos go."

"Did he answer your questions?"

Jinsoo shook his head. "Carlos didn't know why my colleague had become such a monster. I don't know if he was pretending not to know. It didn't look like he was lying to me."

"I'm sorry. I, too, was curious about the full story of what your coworkers went through."

Jinsoo had initially borrowed the detention facility from the governor for the purpose of imprisoning Hogan. The governor also thought it was necessary to find out how Hogan became such a person.

"It doesn't matter. After I wipe out the Union government, I'll ask them directly."

"Did you let him go because he was useless? I wonder. I thought he would kill me."

"I think he might come in handy someday. He's powerful, and it's hard to explain how he's going to do it, but he'll learn the origins of his powers. Inevitably, he'll have doubts about the Planetary Union."

"Do you think he'll convert?

Jinsoo didn't answer.

The governor's doubts turned into certainty. "Is that so?"

"I'm sure he has a lot of reasonable questions thanks to the stories I told him. He's the grandson of Harry Carlos, and Harry Carlos is the commander of the defense of the planetary system that holds the capital and motherland of the Union, meaning, he effectively controls the military power of New Shanghai. Why can't I create a rift between them? Harry Carlos is second to none in this system. Amon Soros cannot be tampered with."

Governor Sakai's expression darkened slightly. "Leader of the Root Restorationists, comrade of the revolution, I have no intention of meddling or modifying your thoughts. But one thing needs to be pointed out for sure."

Sakai spoke low and strong. "Never underestimate the President. You still don't know anything about him and the people around him. The President and his chief of staff, Sura Handler, carefully hold the balance of power in the system. They don't want any cracks. It's no coincidence that Kiliman Ivanov of the Liberal Party was ousted long ago. If Harry Carlos looks like a second-in-command, there is only one possibility: the President is deceiving people for some reason."

Jinsoo thought carefully about Sakai's words. Communication came through his handy tool, and he listened for a while before he spoke.

"The pirates of Valhalla are joining the fleet war now. Maybe the universe will be cleared up soon. It's early, but why don't we all get together after the battle is over? Personally, I've always been interested in those pirates."

Jena opened a comm link with the *Witch Hunter.* "Brother Desmond, it would be good to keep pace with the other ships."

"Are you telling me to slow down?"

"Yes."

"Brother Jena, I've heard of your reputation and respect you very much, but I can't seem to keep up with your words. The battlefield is changing every moment. Once you fall behind, you're bound to collapse. It's just the speed at which they can't respond. We need to get in before they catch on and retaliate."

"Will your ship hold up?"

"I'm sure it will. Trust me, brother." Desmond was confident. "The force field of this ship is stronger than any other ship in the Alliance, brother. I assure you. Trust me."

Jena was silent for a moment, then said, "I know."

The force field wrapped around the *Witch Hunter*'s body. The ship opened its photon gun gate and blew out fire. The Allied cruisers turned toward the *Witch Hunter.* Following behind it, the Brotherhood's assault ships and heavy cruisers fired their guns at the left flank of the enemy fleet. Allied ships were wrecked.

The *Witch Hunter*'s photon cannons fired a burst of light in rapid succession. Desmond drove the *Witch Hunter* through the cracks in the ships hit by the photon guns. The blue stationmaster pushed the Allied ships outward without mercy. It was followed by Jena's assault ship and the others. In an instant, a long blue band was drawn along the spot where the *Witch Hunter* had passed.

Allied assault ships rushed in, but struggled to break through the force field. Meanwhile, the Brotherhood's cruisers and assault ships that appeared from behind the field smashed enemy the ships.

The space carriers that were holding their positions like nodes on the central axis of the left side of the Allied fleet changed direction. Desmond and about ten pirates were considered a threat. As the *Witch Hunter* and the nearest Alliance carrier moved, the battle squadrons changed directions together. It was an instruction from the carrier's bridge. Then a gap appeared that allowed the *Moscow*, which was defending against the attack of the carrier, to advance.

Yuri did not miss the gap. "Get us in there. Now!"

At the same time, all of the *Moscow* warship's guns opened and fired.

The cracks in the Allied lines were getting bigger and bigger.

At some point, the fighter pilot Junkou Meg noticed that the number of Allied fighters flying around him was decreasing. He communicated to his superiors.

"Alpha Leader. Their resistance seems to have weakened.

After a while, the leader said, "The pirates of Valhalla appeared from the side, Meg. Their firepower seems to be dispersing."

"That's great. I thought I'd have to stop at this point, but I think I can keep going now."

"How many planes have you shot down?"

"Five."

"I'm at seven. Let's keep it up."

"I'll see you at closing time, Dallas."

Alpha Leader Dallas laughed.

"All fighter ships from the *Moscow* and the Ganesh fleet , move sharply forward."

A warning popped up on Junkou's dashboard, and Captain Yuri's voice was heard.

"Alpha Squadron, attack the right side of the enemies. Five o'clock position from the main ship.

"Okay, Captain. Alpha Squadron conducting combat maneuvers of the main ship at five o'clock."

Junkou and the rest of the Alpha Squadron opened fire on the Allied fleet ahead of the *Moscow* ship's path. Several fighter ships were destroyed in the Allied counterattack. Junkou clenched his teeth.

He called Haneul Bravo. "Hey, Haneul. I think I'll be terribly tired when I get back, so please take good care of me today. Okay?"

Haneul Bravo heard her lover Junkou's voice and spoke brightly. "Okay, Meg. Don't die. I'll treat you really well."

"Okay. I'm not going to die today!"

Following the Alpha Squadron on the star wap, Yuri watched the situation with fierce eyes.

Haneul said in an anxious voice, "A few aircraft are flying from Ganesh. They seem to be unmanned attack aircraft."

Yuri looked at another part of the star map. A smile appeared on her face.

"Haneul, that's the Ganesh government army. It's the reinforcements sent by Kim Jinsoo."

Haneul's face brightened. Yuri made a quick decision.

"We need to find their command ship, to prevent further casualties for our allies and to end this battle. Haneul, find the command ship in the enemy's camp."

"Yes, Captain!"

When about ten unmanned attack aircraft joined the front line, the Allied forces became much more defensive. Now, the side of the Resistance had an overwhelming advantage. Nevertheless, the Union's firepower had not yet been broken. Karan's fleet attempted to capture the Allied space carriers, but his men were unable to shoot down a single carrier due to surprisingly strong resistance. Yuri wanted not only to lead this battle to victory, but also to minimize sacrifices.

"Captain, it seems there's a space carrier hiding behind the enemy fleet. I found it by analyzing the flow of aircraft signals."

"That's our guy. Karan, let's combine our firepower. We need to capture their command ship."

Karan's voice came through the comm link. "Did you find the command ship?"

"It's a space carrier."

"Okay. I'll go with you, Yuri."

Karan's carrier and assault ship, the *Moscow* warship and the aircraft carrier, and the Ganesh government's heavy cruiser took charge on the opposite side of Desmond's pirates and advanced at once.

It looked like a swarm of bees moving in unison.

Photon cannons, plasma cannons, and rail guns flew along with artillery shells from various places and destroyed the ships. Soon, a huge space carrier behind the combined fleet appeared through the window of the *Moscow* bridge.

Yuri swallowed saliva.

The unmanned attack aircraft flew along the complex calculations of the Ganesh government's control system. Seeing this, Junkou stuck out his tongue. He had thought that humans could exhibit more unpredictable flight than systems. But the unmanned attack planes were using much deeper and more complex movements.

"Alpha Squadron, return to the base."

Junkou was surprised. "Alpha Leader? Come back?"

"Yeah. Our mission today ends here."

"They still have their final carrier, and there are many ships."

"It's the captain's orders."

Junkou made a dissatisfied gesture and let out a grunt. Then he suddenly realized what this meant. "Are they trying to capture their carrier?"

"Yeah, it's land squadron time. They don't need us."

Junkou was amazed. He nodded and turned his fighter to the *Moscow*.

Ship-to-ship capture was virtually impossible in a complex and chaotic battlefield. However, Captain Yuri was trying to win the complete surrender of the Allies through the difficult attempt.

"Captain Ivanova is quite the risk-taker," he muttered to himself.

The *Moscow* warship rushed toward the Allied command line.

In the docking zone behind the *Moscow* ship's air lock, land squadrons in reinforced combat uniforms stood waiting, fully armed. The Discarded's land battle commander Kamura sat quietly with his eyes closed.

He liked this moment. In Kamura's hand was the rail gun he treasured, Death. He clasped and opened his hand, falling into thought.

He went back to his days as a Marine in the ruined Mining Guild.

Twenty years ago, a beam of light fell from the sky and killed people. Soon after, an army of aliens arrived. Kamura, a young soldier in his twenties, looked helplessly at the corpses of his compatriots scattered around the sidewalk blocks. He saw a child who had lost his parents, a woman with bandages, and an old man who looked at him with empty eyes.

The day of the Big Crush.

In his memory, Joshua Kwon, a man who used to be a soldier, approached Kamura, who could not protect his compatriots and was bewildered by the map of hell unfolding in his motherland.

Joshua reached out and told him to destroy their enemies.

Kamura took Joshua's hand. He didn't even realize that tears were running down his eyes.

A fierce vibration shuddered the *Moscow*, jolting Kamura back to reality. The sound of the docking device moving was heard. Soon after came a light clicking sound. Docking device settings, gravity activation, and adjustments were in progress.

Kamura opened his eyes.

It was time to crush and slaughter his enemies.

He looked at his railgun. Then he murmured its name, "Death."

14.

Karan's eyes narrowed as he watched the movement of the *Moscow*. "A fighter! Follow the *Moscow* ship! Never go behind it. When the opportunity arises, it docks!"

After giving those orders, Karan got up and picked up his plasma cutter. Judy followed.

He went to the battle gear storage room by the shortest route from the bridge, found a jumpsuit-type reinforced combat uniform, and pulled it on.

"Captain, are we doing hand-to-hand combat?"

"That's right, Judy. Arm your brothers. Let's go."

"Isn't it better to just shoot them down? So we don't lose more people…"

"Judy. You still don't know our sister? Dear Comrade Ivanova, she intends to subdue them and take their commander directly. And through him, the entire fleet's chain of command will be disrupted and they will surrender. Only seeing the cost of the lives we may lose is an insult to the Brotherhood. We need the loot. That ship could be ours. We'll have to do our part to claim the ship from the Discarded."

Catching on, Judy nodded. He activated the handy tool and ordered all the hand-to-hand combat agents in the fleet to arm themselves. Then, he also found a reinforced combat uniform and changed into it.

The pirates soon gathered behind the airlock. There were more than 100 special forces.

The *Moscow* warship attempted to dock after neutralizing the enemy flagship carrier's defenses. Then, Karan's ship completed the docking.

The docking passages were all connected and the gravity settings were complete.

The docking doors opened, and pirates and Discarded crews poured out from both sides. Facing the pirates, Kamura stopped and looked back and raised his hand. The land crew stopped.

Kamura said with a slight frown to Karan, "I never asked for help, did I?

"I wasn't waiting for your request, Captain Kamura."

"But why are you here?"

"I was just trying to help. You don't like it?"

"Help is accepted with an open mind when the intention is clear, Karan Shetty. For what purpose you set foot on this ship is highly questionable."

Karan smiled and looked into Kamura's eyes with a defiant gesture "I don't plan on cutting our Resistance friends with this cutter, so don't worry, Captain."

Kamura looked at the pirate chief without saying a word, then spoke lowly. "Don't do useless things, and don't get in the way."

Karan only smiled. The pirates and the Discarded land

squadron each entered the enemy carrier from a distance.

The resistance of the Allied forces inside the carrier was fierce. All the soldiers of the Planetary Union were armed and sharpened their rifles. Part of the bulkhead collapsed, crushing several men on both sides. Still, Kamura's land squadrons advanced with overwhelming firepower, and Karan's pirates attacked with great force. Karan, who was at the forefront, wielded a plasma cutter, separating the enemies' limbs and piercing their bodies. Kamura saw it. He was deeply moved by the story of the pirate who used a sword. When he'd first heard the story of the boss of the Valhallan pirates, he'd thought it was a silly joke.

They quickly took control of the ship. The resistance was over, and upon reaching the bridge, the fleet commander they met had a gloomy expression on his face as soon as he saw them.

"You won. Congratulations."

His insignia had two round planets.

"Are you a commander? General? What's your title?"

"I am Admiral Lou Lionel, Commander of the Second Star Mobile Team."

Kamura nodded. "Okay, Admiral. Order the entire fleet to stop resisting."

"And?"

"Those who wish to join us may join us, and those who resist will become prisoners. For those who don't want either, we will provide a ship to return to. But I can't guarantee that there will be enough fuel to get very far. Only God knows if the road out of here is safe."

"It's a stupid question, but what if I say no?"

Karan put a thumb on the admiral's neck. "Don't ask stupid questions."

Kamura glanced at him, then looked at the admiral again. "We will fight to the end. We will also suffer more damage than we have already, but you will all die."

"You're giving us a lot of possibilities, gentlemen. Is that Joshua Kwon's way?"

Kamura shook his head. "This is the way we respect our captain. Otherwise, we would not have kept you alive. Our commander does not want to see any more useless blood loss. Choose, Admiral."

"There's one thing your commander misunderstood."

Kamura gestured as if to tell him, *Go on.*

"The President will not negotiate our ransom after the simultaneous wars you have waged in the Desirée system. Doing so would expose the weakness of the Union government."

"Is that your answer, Admiral?"

The admiral reached into his pocket. The land squadron members and the pirates aimed their guns, but Kamura raised the back of his hand to block their action. Karan looked at Admiral Lou with suspicious eyes.

The admiral took out a cigarette. Kamura didn't stop him. The admiral lit the cigarette, put it in his mouth, and took a deep breath. Karan let out a longing a sigh. Suddenly, he also wanted to smoke.

"I will do as you say," said the admiral. "You have won and we will all surrender. But I have one request."

"What is that?"

"Let me meet your leadership. I have a story to tell."

All the Allied fleet stopped resisting. Mostly were quietly captured by the Resistance forces at the will of their commander. There was some sporadic disturbance and resistance, but it was soon subdued. It was a big win.

Karan asked Yuri to hand over Admiral Lou's carrier to the Brotherhood. Kamura sighed and muttered softly, "I wanted the ship."

Some of the Allied forces joined the Resistance. Most of them were soldiers who came from Ganesh, but some were from the other two planetary systems. Converts from New Shanghai, though, were rare.

Karan Shetty was able to further strengthen the experience of the pirates through the war with the Allied forces. Desmond and Jena also showed excellent leadership aboard their ships, and the Allied assault ships and carriers were secured.

Yuri suggested that the respective commands of the Discarded, Root Restorationists, Ganesh, and Red Wind Brotherhoods meet on the *Moscow* ship to discuss the outcome of the battle and their next plans. Before Kim Jinsoo and Ganesi's governors arrived, Yuri decided to meet with Admiral Lou, who had been escorted to the *Moscow*.

Admiral Lou was detained in a cabin measuring about four square meters. It had toiletries, a bed, and a small table. After a while, Kamura brought him to Yuri's captain's office.

Yuri greeted the elderly admiral. "Hello, Admiral Loui Lionel. I'm the commander of Discarded. Call me Yuri."

"Call me Lou," he said. "I wondered who commanded this battle on behalf of Joshua Kwon. I must say, I wasn't expecting it to be a woman."

"Are you afraid to talk to women?"

"I don't care. I just thought it was an experienced soldier."

"This battle has given me more experience. Take a seat."

She pointed at an iron chair.

The admiral sat down on it. Yuri sat across from him, and Kamura stood in front of the door.

"I heard that you wanted to meet the leadership of the Resistance," she said.

"Can I talk to you?"

"Yes. Do you want to meet someone in particular? The leader of the Ganesh government or the Root Restorationists?"

"It doesn't matter. As long as my story is delivered, that's it." Lou glanced at Kamura. "Why is your friend still here?"

"Captain Kamura is the commander of the Discarded's land battle squadron. And when necessary, he stands as a bodyguard for me or Captain Joshua. You don't have to worry about it."

"I don't care. You can both hear my story."

Yuri thought for a moment and then called Kamura. "Kamura, would you like to sit here and listen to this man's story?"

Kamura turned around and sat down. "I will, Captain."

"Can I smoke a cigarette?" asked Lou.

"That's fine."

Yuri called someone to bring an iron ashtray to her office. Admiral Lou thanked him, then put a cigarette in his mouth and exhaled the smoke. Yuri waited patiently.

"Stop the war," said the admiral. "You cannot win the Union."

Yuri raised an eyebrow. "You're the Union admiral who surrendered to us now."

"I know. Because I wanted to save my men. I wanted to avoid useless sacrifices, too. I also want to pass on a serious warning. Do not bleed into an unwinnable war. You will lose. It will be disastrous."

"Admiral, I think you may know, but Valhalla of the Behemoth planetary system is on our side. The Alliance's Valhalla Mobile Squadron has been shattered, and the ship was secured by us. New Sydney and Neptunus are on the defensive. The first planetary system is at risk, and you have also lost Ganesh in this battle in the second system. Where will it be next? In the third system, Han and Amaterasu still remain, but are they favorable to the Union? It seems that the war situation we are seeing is very different. We cannot guarantee that we will win 100 percent of the war against the Union right now, but it is hard to see how we will lose. Why do you think we will lose, Admiral Lou?"

Lou took a long puff on his cigarette. His blue eyes had a gloomy tint. "What you see is not all of the Allied powers. The President certainly doesn't care whether we win over the Resistance here or not. It's good if we win. Even if we lose, it's just a distraction."

Yuri narrowed her eyes. "What do you mean? You were trying to divert our attention?"

"I know. What the President is doing."

Cigarette smoke increased. When Kamura activated the air circulator in the room, a hum was heard. Yuri looked at Kamura.

"Admiral Lou, do you believe that Amon Soros is up to something, and you think we're not going to win because of it?" asked Kamura.

The admiral nodded.

"And what exactly do you think he's doing?"

"Using things that are not people."

"What did you say?" said Kamura, his brow furrowing.

The admiral removed the cigarette from his mouth,

looked at it silently, and alternately looked at Yuri and Kamura. "I have learned that non-humans exist in this system. And they cannot be killed by human power."

He smiled at Yuri and Kamura's incomprehensible expressions.

"You'll find out one day soon. Perhaps sooner than you think."

Jinsoo was the first to arrive on the *Moscow* ship. He came aboard a small merchant vessel with sub-lightspeed leaping capabilities. Then Governor Sakai came over. Karan showed up with Judy at the end. Kamura led them to the conference room. He told them that the captain would join them soon.

As the people gathered in the conference room one by one, the governor said, "All the heroes that are rising rapidly in the system today, but at the same time giving the Union a headache, are gathered here. Of course, I hope you understand that I understand I am not one of them."

Jinsoo chuckled. "We are still moving forward to be called heroes. However, this bond has only just begun, and although it is not yet strong, I would like to say that the future is much brighter. The removal of the Union fleet from Ganesh is truly encouraging. I hope you will all enjoy the victory, at least for today. And I think the governor is a hero. I believe that his determination played a decisive role in the victory of this battle."

The governor waved his compliment away from a hand. "Whatever you say. Is Captain Joshua still in the alien world?"

"Yes," said Kamura. "Now the captain of the *Moscow* is acting as our captain, and the Wasp is helping us."

"Speaking of, who the hell is Wasp? I've heard that name a lot, but I can't figure it out."

Kamura smiled faintly. "Only our leadership knows who he is. We will know when the time comes."

"You sure do have a lot of secrets," said the governor. "Come to think of it, I don't think I've even heard the captain's name until now. What's his name?"

Right then, the door to the captain's room opened and Yuri appeared.

"Let me introduce myself, Governor. My name is Yuri Ivanova."

The governor made a blank expression for a moment and then looked at her carefully.

"Ivanova? Are you…? No, it can't be…" The governor's pupils widened and his mouth opened weakly. "Are you Kiliman's daughter?"

"Yes." Yuri smiled. " I heard that you were a really good teacher for my sister."

The governor made a sound like a shriek. "I can't believe it! Irina. She is your sister? Did she tell you about me?"

"She did, Governor."

Karan frowned, almost imperceptibly. Jinsoo intervened.

"So, you two know each other?" he asked.

"You know!" said the governor excitedly. "Kiliman and I were close friends. We met while we were in the government. Although we were a little older, we were like political comrades. His eldest daughter, Irina, was my favorite disciple. I'd heard that Irina had a sister." He smiled at Yuri. "So, how is she doing?"

"It's hard to tell, Governor. She's always being chased by the dogs sent by the Union. She's still alive, at least."

"Yeah. Yeah. That's right, Captain. She should be more

careful. I hope she is safe."

Judy, who had been listening quietly, said, "I'm sorry to interrupt when you talk about old memories, but shouldn't we talk about our business now?"

Everyone looked at him. Karan patted Judy on the shoulder and smiled softly.

"As you well know, my friend and I are pirates. We always make it clear what we will receive. I have asked for New Sydney in this war, and in this battle, I have agreed to receive the Allied command ship. Keep that in mind."

Jinsoo threw his arms out in a dissatisfied gesture. "It's not my style to complain about the loot, but the Roots need fleets too."

"If you use that carrier, you will be immediately repulsed by the Allied forces," said Karan with a shrug. "If you want to improve our combat power, it makes the most sense for us to have it."

Jinsoo opened his mouth to argue, but Governor Sakai put a hand on his shoulder.

"Calm down, leader of the Roots. Why are you so bothered? By the way, your craftsmanship is truly amazing, Karan Shetty. I've been wanting to meet you personally for a long time."

"Is that so? Unfortunately, I've never been to, or even paid much attention to, the satellite planet of New Shanghai, since it's mostly a swamp."

Yuri sighed, but the governor laughed.

"Your eloquence is unusual for a pirate. You're right, Shetty. Who cares about this planet? We're practically a gutter of New Shanghai."

Karan snorted.

Jinsoo opened his mouth. "Look, I don't care about the

loot. We should discuss our next plans and get a move on."

" I agree with our leader," said Kamura. "The enemies will attack again. This time, they'll have a much better line-up. We've barely put a dent in Amon Soros's Allied fleet. We need to put a plan into motion before they do."

Yuri considered Kamura's words. "The first planetary system contains New Sydney, and the second system has its mother, New Shanghai, alive and well. The third system has not yet done anything to sympathize with us. It would sure be nice if planet Han would help us, but I fear the probability of that happening is slim."

"So, where to next, Yuri?"

"I don't know yet, but we need to adjust our speed. I have a feeling that if we clash with the Allied forces again like this, the things we accomplished today will no longer matter."

"Then it would be better to prepare for a defense and reorganize the army," said Jinsoo.

Karan looked at Kamura. "Give me the dock, Kamura. It doesn't matter whether yours or in Ganesh. Give me time to reorganize the recently captured ships. I also need time to set up the carrier I've acquired today as my new flagship."

"Everyone seems to agree," said Yuri. "Then, let's reorganize the fleet and strengthen our defense against any future Union attacks. Apart from that, I spoke with Admiral Lou earlier, who is in our custody, and he said something strange." She shared a look with Kamura. "He told me that the Union is creating non-human things. He seemed to think they are the Union's secret weapon."

A groan escaped Jinsoo's mouth. Governor Sakai glanced his way, his face turning rather pale.

"Jinsoo, do you know anything about this?" asked Yuri.

"I have a friend in my crew named Hogan. I sent him and two other crewmembers to Neptunus, where we were told there was a secret Union facility. Only he and one of the others came back alive. But…he's different. The other survivor, Yukyung, said that Hogan should be quarantined indefinitely. Yukyung is undergoing treatment, as well, and we put Hogan in quarantine as she said. Hogan is…very sick."

"What do you mean?" Yuri asked, her brow creasing.

Jinsoo had a hard time getting the words out. "I mean… Hogan wants to attack others."

"Attack?" Karan said.

Jinsoo hesitated. "I don't think he's the person I used to know. He's like…"

"Like what?" pressed Karan.

"He looks like a zombie. A zombie from a horror story."

"A zombie?" Karan clicked his tongue. "I didn't take you for a jokester."

"If you don't believe me, see for yourself. The governor knows what I'm talking about. We locked him up in the governor's facility."

"Then you think Admiral Lou was referring to this comrade of yours?" said Yuri.

"I'm not sure, but maybe so," said Jinsoo softly.

Yuri looked around at everyone and said, "Why don't you all go down with the admiral and show the crew this Hogan in person?"

"Good idea," Jinsoo agreed and stood up. "Will you come join us soon, Yuri?"

"Yes, but first I have some things to clean up of my own. Go on ahead without me for now."

"Will do, Captain," said Kamura. To everyone else, he said, "Come this way."

Most of the group left the conference room. The governor, however, lingered for a moment.

"Now is not the time, but I really want to meet Irina, Yuri," he said.

Yuri smiled. "I'm sure my sister would like to see you too."

"I have a lot of things I really want to tell you. When the right time comes, I'll do it."

After the governor left, Yuri noticed that Karan was still in the room, watching her.

"Karan, are you coming with me?"

"Do you need me, Yuri?"

"I want you to go and see Hogan, too. Let me know what you find out."

"You only want to talk business now." He took a step closer to her. "I'm expecting more than that, Yuri."

Karan grabbed Yuri's shoulder, but she twisted her body away. "Karan, I don't know yet. We're not the same as we used to be."

"Don't say that."

"At least not now. I still have a lot to think about."

"Damn it, do whatever you want." Karan approached the conference room door, but paused and glanced back at Yuri.

"Did you say that the governor was your sister's teacher?"

"That's right."

"I think they were very close."

"He was my father's close friend. My sister told me that he was a really good teacher."

"I think it was more than that."

"What?"

Karan grinned. "Maybe my hunch is right, Yuri. I have a good feeling."

"What are you saying?"

"Nothing, nevermind. See you on the ground then." Karan waved his hand and left the conference room.

15.

Yuri went to a zoo outside the city of Altra as a child. She saw many animals there that she'd never seen in person before. It had been necessary to carefully limit the types and number of animals that were loaded in the limited space on the migration ships. Animals descended from the few individuals selected to preserve the diversity of their species were rare except in New Shanghai. All of them were wandering around the fenced areas helplessly, losing the wildness of their ancestors. They were fragile. Since the migrants hadn't been able to bring the whole food chain of Earth, these creatures could easily die without human care.

"Dad, did anything change from the time when these animals from Earth reached the new system?" asked Yuri.

Kiliman explained kindly to his young daughter. "Well, Yuri, 600 years may be a long time, more than twenty generations for humans, but for the stars, it's a fleeting moment. It's a very short time for a species to change. Although these animals may have evolved into different forms after tens of thousands of years to hundreds of thousands of years, they are not much different than they were when they first arrived in the Desirée. It is the same with us humans. We are still the same human beings, but perhaps tens of thousands of years in the future, we may become different species."

"How many animals did the early migrant fleets carry?" asked Yuri.

"Although the ships were huge, the space for the animals to live was not that big," he said. "Mammals and marsupials, like humans, were frozen, and some brought their eggs. Each animal had no more than four pairs."

"So, all the animals in the Desirée system are kin. Their genetic diversity is on the low side compared to their ancestors on Mother Earth."

"Exactly."

Yuri felt sad as she looked at the animals in the cages. After following humans so far away, nothing had changed for them in the end. The animals were still bred, tamed, and caged.

When she saw an orangutan making a riot at the zoo, she found herself cheering unintentionally. The dark-haired zookeeper said the orangutan had ancestry from a warm country on Earth.

Yuri thought of the orangutan when she first saw Hogan, who was brimming with bloody eyes.

Contrary to the muscles that show the restrained wildness of the orangutan, the twisted limbs and grotesque attachments and joints were not god-like at all.

No one would believe that he was once like us, she thought.

Jinsoo put a finger to his lips. "Shhh. Don't provoke him. He hasn't noticed us yet."

The group stood ahead of Yuri in front of the glass room that held Hogan locked inside. Darkness and faint light blended around them to create a shadow.

Kamura said in a low voice, "Is he really not seeing us?"

"I'll bet. When he sees us, he slams his face into the glass and acts aggressive."

Karan made a harsh sound. "We can't see him properly this way. Why don't you turn on the light and show him to us?"

He started looking for a light switch. Jinsoo grabbed Karan's arm.

"I have the switch."

A light shone on the high ceiling of the hall.

Hogan raised his head and screamed.

Karan said with admiration, "Wow, would you look at that? He sure looks great."

Jinsoo shot him a cold look. "He was my colleague and a wonderful subordinate. I'd appreciate it if you didn't talk about him like that."

"I apologize if I offended you. But this is very exciting, don't you think?"

"Stop it, Karan," said Yuri, walking up to join them. "Admiral Lou, what do you think? Is this the monster you were talking about?"

At Yuri's words, everyone turned to Admiral Lou. Although the admiral had a pale complexion, it was clear that he was exercising considerable restraint. He walked a few steps closer from behind the governor and peered at Hogan through the window.

Hogan banged his head against the glass.

The admiral nodded. "Looks like it. It's similar to the one I know."

"I analyzed Hogan's brain waves, and they looked a lot different from the normal human brain waves," Jinsoo said. "They were quite discontinuous."

"What does that mean?" asked Yuri.

"It means that there is no pattern. In simple terms, it is very different from the brain waves of living things. You may be conscious, but perhaps that consciousness is quite simplistic, unlike humans. You shouldn't expect anything like cognition."

"Admiral, did you see a person like this on Neptunus too?"

The admiral smirked. "Human? Again, this isn't a human. It's a monster. Jinsoo, your colleague isn't here anymore. It's a pitiful and dangerous thing that has lost its reason and has only incomprehensible aggressiveness."

"Why is he quarantined here, Jinsoo?"

At Yuri's words, Jinsoo sadly shook his head. "What could I have done? Should I have killed him right away because he came back like that? I sent him there. We have to find a way to heal him. The other survivor, Yukyung, told me to take care of him, because I could never understand what they went through on Neptunus. It would be better to leave Hogan as he is than to kill him."

"Where is Yukyung?" asked Yuri.

"She's at Ganesh National Central Hospital, though she had to be put into a coma and she hasn't regained consciousness yet."

"Is there any way we could meet with her and ask her some questions?"

Jinsoo shook his head. "No. She needs to calm down. Even if you sent to see her, Yukyung's consciousness won't have returned yet."

"Okay. Let's get out of here for now. Let's talk."

Yuri looked once more at Hogan. It was as if an empty gelatinous mass was staring at her in the place where his eye should have been.

They headed to the room where Jinsoo had served Danny with coffee. Admiral Lou had his handy tools and weapons disarmed, but he walked freely without being bound. Yuri didn't see the need to treat him poorly when she needed his help.

Each of them sat down at a long wooden table. The admiral, Kamura, and Karan were on one side, and Yuri and Jinsoo were on the other side.

Karan said, "I don't know what kind of biochemical weapon the Alliance is preparing, and I don't know what it is, but why not just take Neptunus and New Sydney? I don't see why this needs to be that complicated."

Kamura looked at Karan with a puzzled face. "Were you planning to abandon Ganesh and head back to your planetary system? New Shanghai's fleet is powerful, Karan Shetty. We haven't won the war yet, and Harry Carlos will gather all the forces of the Union and attack us. How many ships do we have?"

Jinsoo had a sad expression on his face. "There aren't many battleships held by the Root Restorationists. Maybe five? Those are older cruisers that no one will care about. We can't do much without the support of the uprising people on each planet."

"The Discarded have twenty or so. Of course, that doesn't include the *Robespierre*."

Jinsoo tapped the table hard with his fingers. "The Ganesh government's Eighth Corps didn't have a mobile squadron. There are a lot of ground troops, but the Ganesh ships are all you've seen. UAVs and about eight ships."

"Then, since there are about twenty Brotherhood ships, about fifty ships make up our strength. Admiral, if the Alliance attacks us again, how large do you expect their fleet to be?" asked Kamura.

The admiral clicked his tongue. "Did you say fifty? The Alliance will bring more than a hundred ships from this planetary system alone. Besides, the number of ground forces is uncountable."

Yuri spoke up. "The one thing I'm still hesitant about is that the sample we've seen right now—I'm sorry, Jinsoo. But to make it easy to understand, there's only one sample: Hogan. Is it smart to bet on something we're not sure about yet? Admiral, what do you have to say about this? What else can you tell us about the Union's secret weapons?"

The admiral took out a cigarette. He searched for a way to light it. Karan handed him a lighter. The admiral narrowed his eyes and looked at the pirate.

"Thank you."

"Can I get one too, Admiral?"

The admiral pulled out a cigarette, looked at it for a moment, and handed it to Karan. "The last one left."

"It's an honor."

"I never thought a pirate would offer me a lighter."

"And I never thought I would get a smoke from an Allied general," said Karan with a chuckle.

Yuri calmly waited for the admiral to continue speaking, as he rubbed the cigarette. Jinsoo, however, was too impatient.

"Give it up, Admiral. We don't have all the time in the

world."

"I was trying to figure out where to begin." The admiral took the cigarette out of his mouth and looked at the leaders of the Resistance. "Maybe it's the work of Sura Handler."

"Sura Handler? You mean the President's chief of staff?"

At Kamura's words, the admiral nodded. "Yes. Sura Handler. Chief of staff of the President. A mysterious figure who suddenly appeared in Union politics one day. Shortly after his appearance, he became the President's right hand and took control of the Parliament. But the President I know didn't have a Sura Handler when he was younger."

"Where is Sura from?"

"He's from Han."

Yuri raised an eyebrow. "Really?"

"I believe so. I don't know the details. His background is all hidden behind a veil. I don't know his age. But it is certain that he was on planet Han during the Big Crush incident. The President sent him for a tax treaty with the government of planet Han. The President always used to say that Sura had gone through the same thing as the people of Han, so he thought he would read them well."

"What does this have to do with zombies?" asked Jinsoo.

"Neptunus was designated as a restricted military area and a base was established after Sura appeared. He is in charge of various secret projects of the Allied forces that even us admirals don't know about. Only he knows what's going to happen."

Jinsoo made a groaning sound.

"If it's all a secret, why do you know about this?" asked Yuri.

"I know because some of my men who were sent to Neptunus in secret did not return. And I've never liked Sura."

"Why?"

"It's just a gut feeling. A lot of strange things have happened since he showed up. Politicians and soldiers who opposed him have disappeared. Those things are not reported by the media within the Planetary Union. But it's definitely true. A lot of the people within the Union have disappeared. One day, neighbors and parents disappear. The next, a small town completely disappears. It's hard to believe, but it's all true. Especially in Ganesh."

Yuri clenched her fists so tightly that her fingernails pierced her skin, causing drops of blood to leak out. She felt dazed.

"Unbelievable things are happening on Neptunus, and they will endanger the Desirée system." The admiral's cigarette shortened. His pupils shook. "It's not common technology. I'm afraid. I'm afraid of Sura Handler and the President. I don't know what they are going to do. But I can be sure, something huge and unknown is coming for us. And I'm sorry, neither the Union nor you will survive that ruin."

"That's ridiculous!" Jinsoo scoffed. "Admiral, you judge and evaluate what you don't understand—"

Karan looked at Jinsoo and said coldly, "He's not finished yet. I'd like to hear more."

The admiral smiled at Karan. "I have nothing more to say. But one thing is certain. There must be some incomprehensible conspiracy behind them."

An alarm sounded from Yuri's handy tool. When she opened the communication port, the ID of Governor Sakai and his face were projected into the air."

"What's going on, Governor?"

"It's an emergency. They're putting the people of Ganesh on ships!"

"What? Are you talking about the Allied forces?"

"Yes. From Nutan Kashmir in the southern hemisphere of planet Ganesh! There are dozens of ships. I don't know why they're taking our people, but I'm calling for a space force right now!"

Yuri looked at Karan. He growled low and connected with the pirates.

"Jena, are you listening? The Union fleet is abducting Ganesh residents. Send the entire fleet with the Resistance."

"Okay, Captain. We just got the news."

Yuri contacted Haneul Bravo in the control room. "Haneul, I need you to get the *Moscow* ready to fly to the coordinates I'm sending you. Let's head to the southern hemisphere of Ganesh immediately after you pick us up."

She cut off communication and hurriedly left her seat. "Everyone, let's go. We'll take a transport plane and fly to the meeting point. Jinsoo, Karan, Admiral, you should get on the *Moscow ship* first."

Yuri and her companions boarded a transport plane and flew straight out of Ganesh City. The transport plane flew for about thirty minutes and soon met up with the *Moscow*. The ship opened its lower dock, and the transport glided inside.

As Yuri watched the transport plane's door open, she asked Karan, "Why didn't Ganesh's air defense system work? How did the Union fleet appear through our defense and surveillance networks like this? Even if they launched the fleet from New Shanghai, it would take a few days for them to get to Ganesh!"

"You already know the answer, Yuri."

"What do you mean?"

Yuri looked at Karan. He didn't say another word. Yuri bit her lip.

"Maybe? Karan, maybe these guys…?"

Karan let out a whistle. "Damn, I don't know how they could have built ships with wormhole navigation devices so quickly, but Nothing can be the answer other than a warp drive! Yuri, you just don't want to believe that right now."

It was true; she didn't want to believe it, because that would change everything.

The southern hemisphere of the planet Ganesh was called Nutan Kashmir. Although the name came from the Indian subcontinent of Kashmir, Nutan Kashmir was quite different. It boasted a natural landscape of mostly dry deserts and steppes, which had a lot of fertile alluvial soil.

Junkou Meg clicked his tongue as he saw the vegetation and the enemy ships appearing through the window. The three giant ships had a long, large oval shape, modeled after the migrant fleet that first arrived in the system.

And the battle fleet of the Union was wrapped around them.

"What a huge transport ship, Leader. Would you believe it even if it was a large migrant ship? It seems that a significant portion of Nutan Kashmir's population has completed boarding."

The Alpha Leader sighed over the receiver. "Then the attack will be difficult?"

"If we attack from the front, it will be dangerous for the residents on board the ship. However, it is not impossible if we suppress their fleet and then attack and neutralize the navigation devices of the other transport ships."

"Okay. I'll report the plan."

After a while, the Alpha Leader spoke again. "The attack has been approved. Subdue their fleet and go straight ahead to find the engine parts of those transports. The battle will be initiated by the cruiser fleet and the attack squadron. We will not directly deal with the fleet, but make a detour with the transports, heading straight ahead. Is there anything you don't understand?"

"No, sir," said Junkou.

The leader nodded. "Okay, begin the maneuver."

The *Moscow* squadron and other Resistance squadrons started the detour maneuver. In addition, the *Witch Hunter* and the *Canberra*, which were deployed on the left wing and the center of the Resistance, centered on a fleet of twenty pirate ships, and started combat maneuvers forward. The right wing was taken over by the Discarded ships.

Photon cannons and plasma started flying through the dry air.

The heavy cruisers of the enemy fleet were destroyed. The planes fell to the same fate.

The Allied resistance was not as strong as expected. Kamura, who was watching the war from the control room, smiled. "I don't think their leadership is firm yet, Captain."

"Seems like it," said Yuri.

"It's clear that they have hastily organized their attack ships."

"Why did the Allied forces target the people of Ganesh?"

"Maybe Admiral Lou knows. Maybe they're trying to distract us?"

"By kidnapping the villagers? Distract us from what?"

"Well, look. The enemy defenses over there are broken. Alpha Squadron is approaching the transports."

Yuri saw the fighters digging into the site where the Allied battleships had been destroyed.

Junkou reported, "Alpha Leader. It's their transport. Based on radio scans, it seems that the engine went through the bulkhead in the center of the rear."

"Okay, all squadron combat maneuvers!"

"It's an unmanned aerial vehicle."

The top outer covers of the transport opened, and drones appeared. Unmanned aerial vehicles rushed into Alpha Squadron, and soon several aircraft maneuvered to evade them. Alpha Squadron tried not to catch the tail. The leader ordered the squadrons in the back row to shoot down the drones following the tailed squadrons.

"Captain! They're pushing us away from the transport."

"I know, Meg. But what other choice do we have?"

Junkou ground his teeth together and departed from the group that was maneuvering to evade the drones.

"Meg. Where are you going?"

"Don't worry about me. I'm aiming for the engines of these transport ships, Dallas."

Junkou's aircraft rotated in place. He moved behind the drones and activated the plasma gun.

The drones collapsed.

Alpha Leader Dallas raised his thumb, guessing Junkou's direction with a spear. "Thank you, Meg. I'll buy you a drink when I get back."

More than a dozen enemy jets followed Dallas toward the transports. Junkou, who shot down a dozen or so in an instant, smiled at the sight.

A loud sound reached his ears. A vibration of unknown origin pierced the sky and spread in all directions.

Junkou's eardrums vibrated continuously. He instinctively recognized that the vibrations had come from the transport ships. His aircraft suddenly tilted. The system went out of control. Junkou's aircraft spun in the air.

Yuri was astonished. "A fighter squadron!"

"Junkou!" Kamura jumped up from his seat and looked over at Sky. Her hands were trembling.

The wings of Junkou's plane broke. The last scene he saw was the small forest beside the meadow growing in his sight.

"The Alpha Squadron has crashed," Haneul Bravo reported in a trembling voice.

"Captain, the land squadron will be dispatched," said Kamura.

Yuri shook her head. "No, Kamura. You've seen all the ships that circled those transports go out of control."

"You're just gonna let them go?"

Yuri opened her eyes and looked at the screen.

"The transports are taking off!" the command and control officer reported.

Open boarding covers of transports closed. The heavy bodies floated up at an astonishing speed. *How can you move so fast?* wondered Yuri.

A blue light came to life in front of the three transport ships that moved leisurely as if they didn't care about the fleet battles going on around them.

It was a wormhole.

Yuri stared at it with widening eyes.

16.

Returning to Altra, Danny headed to Harry Carlos's residence at Alliance headquarters. Harry was waiting for Danny.

"You're back," said Danny said as he sat on the sofa. "You're in uniform. Are you still on duty?"

"It's an emergency."

"After I was imprisoned, I was promoted. Was it you?"

"I couldn't leave the position of the regimental commander empty," said Harry stiffly.

"I will be detained often in the future."

"Don't make useless jokes."

"What about my mother?" Danny asked with a grin.

"Don't worry about your mother. I don't know about her. She probably thinks you're still in Ganesh."

Danny put on an absurd look on his face. "Didn't you tell her what happened?"

"Nilla would have had a heart attack had she known about this. Damn it, tell your mom that Danny Boy was

kidnapped and imprisoned? I'd rather do some cold weather training."

"You're such a grandpa."

Danny smiled bitterly. His mother, Nila, was a delicate
woman. It'd been said that she had been like this since
her husband, Sean, came back from Han and went half
crazy. But Danny thought his mother must have been a
weak-hearted girl from a much younger age.

He thought of Sean Carlos. A young and energetic man
he could only remember through photos and videos. He
wished he could talk to his father at least once. He thought
he would get along well with the younger Sean Carlos.
Now Danny was about the same age as Sean before he
died.

Sean.

Father.

What did you see on planet Han that day? Danny wondered.

"Did they treat you unfairly?" asked Harry.

"No. I met Jinsoo Kim, but he wasn't a mean person."

Harry took a beer from the fridge and threw it at Danny. Danny caught it and opened the can.

"What did he say to you?" asked Harry.

"It wasn't a big deal. He said something funny. That
the Union government had something to do with the Big
Crush. What do you think, Grandpa?"

"I don't know what you mean."

Danny looked at Harry's complexion, but Harry didn't
show the slightest agitation. "He is from Han, grandfather.
We all know that Han people have a lot of problems these
days. He was very confident that the Union government
caused the Big Crush. Why would Jinsoo Kim think that

way?"

"What else did you talk about?"

"He said that Uncle Yeonsu understood them, and that I would understand them too."

Harry snorted. "Gibberish."

"Are there any stories you haven't told me?"

"Danny."

"I want to know what happened on planet Han twenty years ago. The whole story. From start to finish, Grandpa."

Harry opened and then shut his mouth.

"Obviously, there are some things that are not quite clear," continued Danny. "There have been a few times when alien merchants appeared in our system. They knew that humans existed. But they attacked as soon as human ships arrived in their world? Why were they so aggressive? Unexpected aggression. In part, Kim Jinsoo is right. There are stories that are not known to the public. And he said that my grandfather would know those stories."

Harry looked at Danny without saying a word.

"Grandfather."

Danny tried to grope for something hidden behind Harry's eyes. But the more he looked, the emptier his grandfather's eyes appeared.

"What on earth do I not know? Why did Uncle Yeonsu leave us?"

Harry drank the beer. A bitter taste ran down his throat.

Several scenes overlapped in his mind.

Skeletons. A scene from the frenzy that swept through Harry's childhood. The whimpering children gathered together, dying with fearful eyes. Harry saw the body of a man who had been slayed.

It was his father, who was killed by an angry crowd

because he had inherited last name. Later, Harry found out that the day he was killed was what people called the Second Name War.

Gibberish.

It was just a massacre.

Harry saw another scene. Collapsing rubble. Burnt and scattered corpses. Residents who lost their lives to the alien attack.

It all looked like that. The beginning, middle and end of his life. The images that ran through his memory were all the same.

"It's all in vain," he said.

"Yeah?"

"The things you ask, these stories you want to hear. It's all in vain, Danny."

Danny shrugged as if he didn't understand.

Harry drank a beer. "You must have listened to me a lot. Stories of how I lost my parents as a child to those damn 'Nameless.' Danny, your great-grandparents. They weren't going to die like that. And twenty years ago, I saw and experienced the Big Crush firsthand. I directly suppressed the revolt of the Valhallans who refused to join the Union ten years ago. Danny, what do you think I must have been thinking as I watched and experienced all these things? What kind of thoughts do you think your grandfather would have had when he lived in such a world?"

Danny looked at Harry Carlos, an old soldier and politician. He thought about the curves hidden behind his grandfather's stubborn forehead and deep eyelids.

"I realized that destruction, slaughter, and war are human destiny. No matter how old the universe gets, that doesn't change. Our ancestors did it on Earth, and they did it when they came here. How many small and large wars have occurred since humans settled in the Desirée system? As many as 1,000. War is inevitable and the law of the flow of history, Danny. How ephemeral it would be to give meaning to each and every one of them."

"Grandpa, you can't just ignore the truth—"

"Danny, the truth, whatever it is, will eventually be forgotten in the great flow of history. Do you know what the only truth is?" Harry laughed. It was a laugh full of dust, accompanied by a lackluster smile. "It is the fact that humans desire self-destruction."

"Oh, yeah?"

More laughter erupted from Harry's mouth. His diaphragm shook and his insides vibrated to the point of itching. A powerful laugh ran through his toes and then climbed over his head. It felt like an intolerable emotion was expelling through every hole in his face.

Seeing Harry grinning, Danny raised his hands and lowered them. It was the first time he'd seen his grandfather like this. A man with the military power of the star system was laughing with tears in his eyes.

Harry shrugged and wiped the tears away. "Danny, Danny. You damn bastard. Let's stop talking about this. What the hell did you hear? Even you. Huh?"

Danny didn't say anything.

"I've already lost Sean, your father, and now Yeonsu has abandoned me too. Danny, are you like your father and uncle? Tell me you aren't. Please."

Harry Carlos grabbed his grandson by the shoulders. Danny could feel his rough breathing. He could feel his solid power still moving alive.

"Don't say such nonsense anymore. I don't want to talk

about it any more. Okay?"

"Grandfather—"

"Stop." Harry let go of his shoulders and drank the beer again. "A guest will come here tomorrow. Someone you've never seen before. He wants to meet you."

"What guest?"

"The President."

Harry smashed the can of beer in his fist.

End of Book One

Author's Note

It is great to share my stories with readers outside my home country. Born in Far East Asia and a student of English Literature, it has been my lifelong dream. I hope that all of you Science Fiction fans have enjoyed this book.

A lot of things happened when I was creating and writing this book, but now the world is buzzing with COVID-19. Humans are interconnected, and it will be the same when pioneering the universe. I don't know what you think about my home country. I personally believe that this book is closely related to the political situation and location of my home country as a whole. The artist cannot be free from the circumstances and backgrounds of the times he is in, and I believe that it is sublimated into his own unique perspective. This book, naturally, contains my perspective.

My home country is not a normal country. The size of the country is similar to Florida, and you can experience both the extreme weather of the Northern Hemisphere and the heat of the Southern Hemisphere.

Geopolitically, it is currently the only divided country in the world. Here, a country with a democracy and advanced economy, which is rare even in Asia, and a dictatorship with a tyrannical system that is hard to find in human history coexist within a small country. This country is also an ally of the United States of America. In neighboring countries alone, there are countries with the second and third largest GDP in the world, and Russia, the successor of the Soviet Union.

Culturally, in the past it was the intersection of the continental and maritime cultures of Chinese civilization and nomadic peoples, and it was a location that became a bridgehead for each civilization.

What I want to say is that people in my culture, including myself, have a lot of stories they really want to tell the world. But with our isolated locations and circumstances, we have never had many opportunities to tell the world our story. Most of you in the Western world have probably heard our story through the perspectives of Chinese and Japanese people. So, I wanted to tell you our voices, our fears, and concerns in the form of a space opera.

A novel is a mirror that predicts the future. As a Korean, I projected my fears as a citizen living next to a unified giant country in my writing, but perhaps this is an emotion that all mankind will feel in different times and spaces. I hope that one day all humans can think of them as if they were from the far distant past. I also hope that one day we will go beyond the limits of our mortality and think beyond the nebula.

I wrote this book with the fun of daydreaming in the hopes that we can someday travel between nebulae and stars. Dreaming up the future of all mankind is not a small thing. Thank you again for taking the time and read my book.

About the Author

Min Hyesung majored in English Literature and Political Science. He is interested in the manifestation of the human nature and the inhuman reality in situations and in human eras, and the story of the human being in those situations and eras, and would like to realize this in literature. He is planning various works across several genres, such as sci-fi, fantasy literature, and hard-boiled.